THE THRONE IV

COLE HART

CONTENTS

The Throne IV

Mailing List

To stay up to date on new releases, plus get information on contests, sneak peeks, and more,

Go To The Website Below...

www.colehartsignature.com

BOOKS BY COLE HART:

I'm Just Tryin' To Be Somebody's Wife

The Sunday School Teacher

The Sunday school Teacher II

I Need A Fiancée Like Beyonce

I Like My Women BBW

Rich Thugs

The Throne

The Throne 2

The Throne 3

The Throne 4

The Plug

The Plug 2

Godfather of Atlanta

Godfather of Atlanta 2

Red Bottom Bitches

Red Bottom Bitches 2

Red Bottom Bitches 3

Drunk In Love: An Original Love Story

Drunk In Love 2: An Original Love Story

Drunk In Love 3: An Original Love Story

Drunk In Love 4: An Original Love Story

Crazy Summer

Bow Tie Mafia

CONTACT THE AUTHOR:

Facebook: Cole Hart
Facebook Author Page: Author Cole Hart
Instagram: @authorcolehart

COLE HART PICASSO:

When I wrote The Throne I, was telling any and all haters to close their eyes and imagine me as being John Coffee from the movie The Green Mile. I also stated to y'all to allow me to remove that nasty disease called HATE from your body so that I can take it into mine. Well since then, the actor who played John Coffee has passed away, and I've had a change of Hart... Damn it's a Cole World and I'm not talking about a J Cole Album. Real Talk, I was willing to save you and remove your hate a few months ago, but I really realized that without y'all, it wouldn't be no me and all these fire stories that I write. Without y'all, it wouldn't be no BankrollSquad and the strength and loyalty behind our team. Without y'all, it wouldn't be no Write House Publishing. Without y'all, it wouldn't be a lineup of sub companies under SBR Publications. Without y'all, we wouldn't have the best team of writers and authors under one umbrella. Without y'all, my brother David Weaver wouldn't have nobody to flexx on with them 6 figure checcs, and I definitely wouldn't have nobody to talk ish to.

Yeah, I know it's probably some people sitting bacc reading this and saying, Cole Hart is so arrogant. Well just make sure you add the word CONFIDENT to that as well. Matter of fact, I'm so arrogant and confident that I just might change my name to Cole Hart Picasso after this book. However, I'll let my readers and fans be the judge of that after they read this one.

Moving on, allow me to thank God first and foremost for blessing me with the many talents to write and publish and my creative style and ambition. In 1999, I was handed a life sentence for being about that so called life. I dropped out of school in the 9th grade, but I only had an 8th grade education until I came to prison. I never was dumb or nothing, I was just caught up in the streets since I was fourteen years old, and I actually didn't care because school wasn't feeding my family. That was my attitude at the time. So this journey that I've been on from the streets to the penitentiary has been nothing more than a blessing from the man above. God.

Allow me to thank my family and my BankrollSquad family for keeping me on my toes and keeping me driving and definitely riding with me on this journey. To my editor, Tina Nance, thank you for all the hard werk you put in on all four parts of The Throne series. I salute you for that.

Big shout out to all the authors that's signed with Write House. Just know we definitely running up the checc for 2014, and I'm just being honest. More zeroes and extra commas coming soon for everyone. Well I'm not gonna bore y'all any further, except to ask y'all to keep me in your prayers. Stay blessed.

Sincerely Yours,

Cole Hart Picasso... Yeah, I like the sound of that.

PROLOGUE

New York City is cold. That is one of the first things that comes to mind when someone from the south thinks of The Big Apple. Second, are the tall buildings, the skyscrapers, and the Statue of Liberty. The city always seems to be moving. This particular day wasn't very cold, and the sun was bright and blazing high above Manhattan. The sky was a crisp blue. From the third floor of a high-rise building in downtown Manhattan, the DEA and ATF had a full-scale surveillance in progress on a young notorious team of killers and drug dealers. The feds had dubbed their crew The Picasso Money Gang. They sponsored local rappers in the city of New York only. They were rumored to be associated with the Jews, and even had a Russian connect through the underworld of New York, and beyond.

The feds had estimated their money take in at nearly fifteen million a week, but they were off by a long shot. It was more like fifty million a week; they just had a lot of mouths to feed. In reality, they were moving weight by the tons.

On the stakeout that afternoon, there were four agents. Two from the DEA and two from the ATF. Four white males, clean-shaven and comfortably dressed in jeans, tee shirts, vests and running shoes were on the team. They had one long fold out table sitting directly in front of the window, which looked down at one of the most expensive and respected studios in New York. The agents had high tech cameras and other surveillance equipment aimed out the open window. Through a pair of binoculars, one of the agents could see young looking Arabian women dressed with their heads covered and thin-dark veils covering the lower half of their faces.

The streets were busy. A homeless man was standing about thirty yards away from the Muslim women. He looked spaced out and he walked with a limp. The federal agent moved his binoculars back to the Muslim women; they were in good deed, selling oils, fruit, fresh scented candles, pies, and a few more items. He surveyed the block from every angle. Nothing seemed out of place.

The task for the day was to get a couple of pictures of the targets in their new fancy cars. As if on cue, from the right, just behind two black Ninja motorcycles, four black on black Bugattis appeared, million dollar sports cars.

The federal agent pushed his New York Mets fitted cap off his head and snapped his fingers to gain the other three agents' attention.

One of them was eating a turkey sandwich on Rye; he dropped it back on a Styrofoam tray, brought up his camera, and aimed the nose through the slit of the curtain. His lens immediately landed on the Bugattis; they were glossy black and clean. All four of the cars were just easing up to the curb. Another agent pulled out a mini camcorder and the third pulled out his camera.

Something happened right before their eyes that they never expected. The Muslim women brandished mini assault rifles from underneath their hijabs. The bum that had been walking with the limp took out the two guys riding the Ninjas, and then major gunfire erupted.

The agents couldn't believe what they were seeing. This was an ambush. One of the agents got on his radio immediately and called for backup. He then scrambled to his feet, adjusted his vest, and checked his weapon. "I'm going in." He yelled as he took off toward the elevator.

The agent and his partners aborted their surveillance and joined the live action playing out on the street.

BOOK 1

1

It was quiet in the rear of the limousine, as Papa Bear desperately tried to repress the thought of how they'd just escaped the feds by only inches. He was used to danger, but that was a narrow escape, even for him. He would do it all again in a heartbeat, to be in this moment with Falisa lying in his arms.

As Falisa tried to relax, something flashed through her; a terrible feeling that she couldn't quite put her hands on. She leaned over and looked through the tinted window at the passing cars. Squinting, she tilted her head and checked the sky. The passing palm trees seemed to be slowing, and in a chain reaction, it seemed that their limousine was slowing down as well. A feeling of panic washed over her.

Papa Bear pulled out a bottle of Pernod Ricard Perrier Jouet champagne and popped the top.

Falisa accepted her champagne glass and a smile spread across her face. Champagne spilled from the mouth of the bottle as Papa Bear poured Falisa a glass. He handed it to her and then poured himself one. He set the bottle down in the cabinet and held up his glass. Falisa did the same thing.

They hooked their arms around each other, and before they sipped, she said, "To our new beginning."

"To our new beginning."

Their glasses clinked in a light melodic tone, and then they sipped from their glass.

Falisa smiled and tried to ignore her gut feeling that something wasn't right.

Papa Bear was also uncomfortable; he felt the car slowing down himself.

The limousine abruptly jerked, as if the driver had slammed on the brakes. The sound of a helicopter hovering just above them filled the space.

Papa Bear turned and looked out the tinted window on his side. Falisa followed suit. Nervousness washed over her entire body. They weren't looking for her, couldn't be. *Not now. Oh my God, this can't be happening now.* She silently said to herself. Her hands trembled as she turned her champagne glass up to her lips and drained it in one gulp.

The limousine finally came to a complete stop.

Papa Bear slowly leaned forward and set his glass inside the cabinet. His movements were deliberate and cool. Whistling softly, he refilled Falisa's glass before he picked up the assault rifle and tapped the partition with the barrel.

The driver of the limousine pressed a button on the door panel and rolled down the glass. His eyes met Papa Bear's through the rear view window.

Papa Bear saw in his eyes that something was terribly wrong.

The driver then put the limousine in park. They were on a side street with palm trees lining both sides. "We are surrounded, sir... ma'am." And without another word, he politely stepped out and left the limousine running.

Papa Bear was speechless, and his mouth was slightly parted. At least the driver had closed the door behind him.

Outside, the sky was bright and clear; the hot Florida heat had dried up the earlier rain showers. The team of federal agents caught on quickly. They knew there was no way possible that Falisa had gone very far.

The limousine that Papa Bear and Falisa was sitting in was bulletproof and had dark tinted windows, but none of that mattered, because they were surrounded by at least two dozen armed federal agents. From the inside, Papa Bear locked all the doors.

Falisa was watching them from inside as she sipped her champagne. She was more relaxed now, just a little bit, though. She didn't know if this was her last stop or not. What she did know, was the she wasn't ever trying to visit another prison cell. Her current options appeared to be limited. She pictured them riddling her body with bullets and loading her inside a black body bag. She closed her eyes for a brief moment, lost in her own thoughts.

Just outside the limousine, federal agents in dark suits and ties were circling the car, trying their best to see through the dark tints. More agents in blue DEA jackets, jeans and boots were out there as well. They were laughing and joking, and some were tapping their badges and guns against the glass.

Papa Bear took a deep breath and rubbed his hand over his face. To his surprise, when he looked over at Falisa, a small smile danced across her lips.

"Any suggestions?" he asked her.

Without a word, Falisa flipped open the inside panel box and clutched the car phone. She punched in a number, and three rings later, she heard Amil's voice on the other end.

"Hey Mother."

Falisa held her breath. Her eyes darted around, between the agents outside and Papa Bear sitting calmly beside her.

Finally, she spoke into the phone. "Things are not looking good for your mother." She sighed.

"Where are you?"

"Surrounded by a hundred federal agents in a limousine off of I-95."

There was a long silence, then a loud tap from one of the agents outside made Falisa jump.

"Don't panic. Let me see if I can get you out of this."

"We're on a thin line, Amil." Falisa said, and held her glass out toward Papa Bear.

He refreshed her drink and gave her a warm smile. He appeared calm, but he was nervous as hell for Falisa. Even with a fully automatic assault rifle, there was still only so much that he could do. At best, he would get off a couple of rounds, and then he'd be gunned down along with Falisa.

"Don't judge me, Mother. Talk to you later."

The call ended before Falisa could respond. She was on pins and needles, sipping her champagne to ease her pains. Her mind began moving in many directions. *Ain't no motha fuckin' way*. She thought. Then from the outside, they heard a male voice echoing from a bullhorn.

"Turn off the car and step out."

Falisa eased closer against Papa Bear and locked her fingers inside his. There was nothing else to hide at this point. Now they waited.

Outside, a federal agent stood on the hood of the limousine, a white guy with a shiny bald head and a thick mustache. He was very aggressive looking; his eyes were hidden behind a pair of dark shades and he wore a tight fitting vest over his upper body. Just behind him, one of the head agents stood near the hood of a blue Suburban. He was dressed in a two-piece suit, a shirt and tie. His hair was black and oiled down toward the back.

The handsome agent's name was Paul Edgar. He wore his cellphone on his waist, and when it vibrated, he answered it immediately. "Agent Edgar speaking."

"Hello, Mr. Edgar, my name is Amil Walker. I am the daughter of Falisa Walker, the lady that you have right there in the limousine. I'm also the daughter of Timothy Walker. He is dead, by the way, and I'm the only person who knows where his remains are." She paused. "Are you listening?"

"With both ears," he said.

"Good, here's the deal. I'll give you the location of Timothy Timbo Walker's body. Also, I'm sure you all are still looking for Iris James. Well, for one, she's changed her face, but I can also give you her. She's alive and well, and closer than you think. Also, your star witness that was hiding out in Toronto, Canada, with his mother and grandmother. I'm responsible for their deaths. The four bodies that were found in the trunk in Missouri a couple years ago; I'm responsible. Today, within the next hour, I'll turn myself in and give you everything and everybody that I just named, if you let my mother go right now."

Agent Edgar stood there dumbfounded for a minute while he took in all of the information. Then he said, "Ma'am—"

Amil cut him off. "Listen, you have to reason with me. If you hesitate, that'll make me nervous. I just sent you a family portrait to your phone. It should be coming through now."

Agent Edgar looked at his smartphone, and just as sure as shit stinks, a new text message had just come through. He touched the screen, entered his password, and touched the icon for the new message. When he opened the attachment, there was a photo of his wife with terrified eyes and a strip of duct tape over her mouth. His daughters, one nine years old and the other fourteen were beside their mother, wearing identical horrified expressions with duct tape also covering their mouths. The terror in their eyes was like they'd all seen the same ghost.

Agent Edgar's heart stopped. The situation had just turned serious as cancer. Any thoughts he had about this being a feeble attempt by Falisa to avoid capture faded fast. He put the phone back to his face. A lump formed in his throat. "I'm listening."

"Let them go, everybody come on back to the sanatorium. You'll get me and Iris, and even better, you'll get your family back in one piece. That's my word."

Agent Edgar held the phone and stood in silence. He couldn't make a call like this without solid reasons. His eyes scanned his men that were standing around the limousine with their weapons drawn. Then the photo of his family flashed in his mind again.

"Miss, I suggest you let my family go and—"

"I'm trying to reason with you here, Mr. Edgar." Amil's tone changed from polite to deadly. Then, she said casually, "So, I'll assume you don't value your family. I'm not trying to resort to violence. I just sent another pic to your phone. After you look at it, hang up and leave. I'm waiting."

The line went dead.

Agent Edgar looked at his phone once more and touched the message icon. The image of his mother and father on their knees with their hands tied behind their backs and each of their mouths covered with a silver strip of duct tape appeared. But what scared agent Edgar even more, was the two men standing behind his parents. Their faces were covered with masks, and shades hid their eyes. They each held large blade knives to his parents' necks.

Agent Edgar briefly closed his eyes and pondered the situation at hand. He had no choice. On his orders, everyone cleared out and headed back to the sanatorium. With his cellphone still in his hand and his heart in his stomach, he climbed in the driver seat of a dark blue Suburban and punched the gas with blue lights blazing. The convoy was right behind him.

2

_____

Papa Bear watched the band of federal agents load into their cars. Falisa was watching from her side window, still holding her glass of champagne, and nearly holding her breath at the same time. For some reason, they were taking off in the vehicles, but the helicopter was still hanging around.

Without warning, Papa Bear climbed into the front seat and shifted the car into drive. Falisa was smiling now. She didn't know what her daughter had said or done, but so far, it was working.

Just as Papa Bear was slowly moving their limousine out of the roadblock and the jam of cars, the phone rang.

Falisa picked up. "Yes?" she answered. Her eyes scanned the expressway through the tinted window. They were moving now.

"Mother, I need y'all to go to the warehouse." The line went dead.

"To the warehouse." Falisa said with the phone still pressed against her face.

Papa Bear's eyes found hers in the rearview. He was serious

again, and his look spoke volumes to her. They knew some undercover agents were still following them and riding incognito in something unrecognizable. But they would play their part and move accordingly.

AGENT EDGAR DROVE like a bat out of hell, trying to make it back to the sanatorium. On his cellphone, he called Quantico and spoke with his boss. He immediately gave him the rundown about the situation with his family and Amil Walker calling him directly on his phone.

"I'm sending someone out to your family now and to your parents' house as well. For now, comply with their demands. If they're in the sanatorium now, there is no way they can leave without being apprehended. Try to keep them alive."

He hung up, and then he called straight through to the commander of the federal SWAT team, who was already at the sanatorium. An anxious and deep voice answered. "Yes."

"Special agent Edgar speaking. Listen, from my understanding, we may have two still there in the sanatorium somewhere. Seal the entire place off, and I'm on the way. We must keep them alive."

He hung up again and pressed the pedal to the floor.

BACK AT THE SANATORIUM, federal agents combed the place, searching for the criminals. The coroner was loading the nurse's body inside a black body bag and then on to a gurney. They would take her back and run an autopsy to clarify the cause of death. The SWAT Team went room to room, not leaving a door unlocked or a rock unturned.

When Agent Edgar arrived, he went straight inside through

the front entrance, past the thick yellow tape. As soon as he got inside, his cellphone went off again. He pulled it out and answered it.

"Edgar speaking."

"Hello, this is Amil Walker again. Now just like I said earlier, I'll surrender and I'll give you Iris James once I know my mother is safe and isn't being followed. To assure my word, I'm downstairs in the throne room. You'll have to take the service elevator downstairs to the basement."

Agent Edgar snapped his fingers at the team of agents. All eyes were immediately on him. Then he said into the phone, "And how do I get to the elevator?"

Amil guided him from the phone. They walked through the place, found a door, and went through it. As a unit, they moved down the corridor with guns drawn and ready. All of them were highly trained and professionally skilled. The elevator was to their left. Some of them looked around for a staircase exit, but there was none. The SWAT commander whispered into the team earpiece, informing them of their progress.

Five agents packed themselves inside the elevator with the MPS AA-12s ready. Agent Edgar came in last, still with the phone against his face.

"We're inside the elevator," he said to Amil on the phone.

"Good." she said." Basement floor."

He pressed the button, and then he moved toward the back of the elevator. The SWAT officers waited for the destination. The elevator jerked a little and the doors parted open, revealing a corridor with double doors at the end.

The SWAT was out and combing the area with guns drawn and infrared beams waving in every direction.

"We're here, on the basement floor standing in front of two huge wood doors."

"Okay, excellent. Now, we'll have a standoff like on TV until I know my mother is safe."

Two members of the SWAT team was already removing small pin like cameras. They inserted one underneath the bottom of the door and with luck and faith, they actually saw Amil standing in the middle of the floor with the phone pressed against the side of her face. They shifted the small camera, and there was another woman who they assumed was Iris. She looked worried, but she was sitting there like a duck, just staring off into space. They watched them from a hand held device.

The SWAT commander looked up at Agent Edgar. "There's two women inside. Alive."

Agent Edgar pulled out his walkie-talkie and radioed in to the agents that were following the limousine by helicopter.

"Abort mission, back off the limousine." was all he said. Then he spoke into the phone to Amil. "My end of the deal is handled. Now open the doors so we can get this over with."

3

———

P apa Bear drove on I-95 south, he was definitely nervous, more anxious than anything else. The phone rang in the rear of the limousine and Falisa picked up immediately. "When you get to the airport in Miami buzz this line back." Amil said, and then the line clicked again.

Amil was making her nervous. Falisa peeped out the window; the helicopter was out of sight, as far as she could see. Then she said to Papa Bear, "Change of plans. We're going to Miami international."

Papa Bear eyed her from the rearview. His head nodded one quick time and his head and eyes went straight back to the cars ahead of him.

Falisa looked over to where Papa Bear had left the AK. She reached over and pulled it closer towards her as she took a deep breath to relax. Then she took the remote control and pressed the power button for the TV. She flipped the channel to CNN, and there was her old spot covered with SWAT, Feds and local authorities. EMT was there and several news reporters. Falisa picked up the champagne bottle and filled her glass again. For the next twenty minutes, they rode in silence, by passing Ft. Lauderdale and quickly making their way into Dade County.

Almost another thirty minutes went by before they arrived at Miami International. Papa Bear drove around, slipped the limousine under the parking deck, and parked. Falisa picked up the phone and dialed Amil's number, but she didn't get an answer. That made her worry a little. She knew Amil was on point, and ten steps ahead, but she also knew that when it came to the Feds, their options were very thin and limited. She hung up the phone and waited anxiously for whatever was going to happen.

Out of nowhere, twin Hummers pulled up back to back, both of them cocaine white with tinted windows.

The SUVs blocked them in, and the passenger side window on the Hummer in the rear lowered. The face of an older looking Arabian man appeared. He leaned out the window with his head wrapped in a headdress that is sometimes referred to as a turban, and extended his arm.

Papa Bear stepped out of the limousine and quickly opened the back door for Falisa.

The rear door of the Hummer opened and Falisa and Papa Bear walked straight toward it and got inside.

THE SWAT TEAM, Agent Edgar and several other federal agents had Amil and Iris boxed inside the throne room. Agent Edgar's cell phone buzzed again. "Yes." he answered.

"I guess this is it." The line went dead.

The locks clicked from the inside the throne room, and within two seconds, all the SWAT members were locked and loaded. The agent in the front twisted the door handle and slowly pushed it open. The room was dimly lit, and Amil and

Iris both stood thirty feet away with their hands high above their heads.

"Down on your knees." the first SWAT member shouted.

Amil and Iris moved at the same time, dropping down to their knees as the agents rushed toward them. When the first SWAT member got close to them, something didn't seem right. He reached down and realized that Amil and Iris were only hologram images. He waved his hand through the image; he couldn't believe it. Someone hit the lights, and both images faded away into thin air.

Agent Edgar laughed half-heartedly. "A fucking hologram."

He put his hands on his waist and stared around the high ceilings and walls in total disbelief. Then he picked up his phone and dialed his home number. While he waited for someone to answer, his heart fell deeper into the pit of his stomach. It rang once... twice... On the third ring, someone picked up and his hands began to tremble.

"Hello..." his wife's voice rang through the phone. She sounded cheerful as can be.

What the hell? He took a deep breath and asked, "Is everything alright?" Where's the kids?"

While he waited for her to respond, his stomach twisted in painful knots.

Then she responded. "Yes sweetheart, everything is alright here. The kids are fine. We're here baking cakes for the girl's school tomorrow. What's wrong? You sound worried."

Agent Edgar cleared his throat and found his voice. With one hand, he loosened his tie and let it drape around his neck.

"Umm... nothing. Just keep the doors locked. There's gonna be a couple of agents coming by, nothing to panic about, okay. Now let me get back to work. Kiss the kids for me."

"Okay, honey. Love you." She chirped happily from the other end.

Agent Edgar hung up and immediately dialed his parents'

home number. The phone rang three times before his father's voice came through the phone, loud and clear.

"Edgar residence."

He could've cried when he heard his father's voice. He tried his best to conceal his smile, but he couldn't.

"Hey Dad," he said, and turned his back to the rest of the agents.

"Is everything alright?"

"Yes, son, everything is fine here. Your mother is out in the garden. She says the worms are eating her tomatoes again. Anyway, I'm bored and playing chess online."

Agent Edgar bit his bottom lip. Not hard, but he was clearly relieved to hear that his parents were safe and hadn't been touched.

Edgar was a top federal agent who played by the rules to the best of his ability. He was definitely a major player on the field. Moments after he hung up the phone with his father, he slowly turned around in a circle, nodding his head and visually taking inventory of throne room. He observed the high cathedral ceilings with the artwork of Angels and Devils fighting with swords suspended in mid-air. *Who are these people?* he asked himself. Then his eyes went to the huge throne chair, the long blue carpet and the gold lion statues that were lined up. All of this would be etched in his memory. While the rest of the Federal agents were going through the place with a fine tooth comb, he looked back at his phone to view the photos again, and to his surprise, they'd vanished.

He only shook his head as he realized that he was the joke.

From the left side of him, another agent yelled out, "Yeah fellas, we got high-tech quality cameras that display and enable three-dimensional images. They're set up from all four cameras."

All the agents looked in the direction that he was pointing.

"Holography," Agent Edgar said. "Interference diffraction."

"Clearly, we're dealing with some very rich and smart people here."

That alone made Agent Edgar even thirstier. "Amil Walker," he said softly. "You can guarantee I'll see you in the future. That's my word."

And he would.

DUBAI-UAE

4

I t was dark outside, but from Falisa's window on the huge private jet, the sight of the beautifully illuminated Dubai skyline rendered her speechless. Papa Bear was sitting across from her, flipping through a *Condé Nast Traveler* magazine that featured the opulent lifestyle of Dubai, including the many mansions, palaces, exclusive hotels and vacations spots that the city offered.

"This city is beautiful." Falisa said, still staring out the window in disbelief and wondering to herself how in the hell Amil managed to form a relationship with the Arabs. *Well, one things for sure, we're gonna find out when we land.* Falisa decided. She was still somewhat worried about her family. Her eyes shifted to Papa Bear, she studied him briefly as he flipped the pages of the magazine. He was in a silk shirt with buttons down the front, cool linen pants, and expensive boat shoes.

Feeling Falisa's eyes on him, he lifted his eyes from the magazine and met her gaze. "How you feeling?" He asked her as he closed the magazine and set it on the marble table between them.

Falisa smiled. "We left them bastards nearly a billion in

cash back there." She said and shook her head. She wasn't stressing at all about the money, because she knew she'd get it back some way

Papa Bear nodded his head in agreement. "Once we get ourselves situated and settled in, you can best believe we'll make a major come back." He turned and glanced out the window. Dubai was by far, the most beautiful city in the world.

The jet landed at Dubai International, and before it stopped, they could see four black Hummers racing on either side of them. The jet was carefully guided inside a well-lit private hanger, where it came to a complete stop.

Immediately, several Arabs spilled out from the Hummers. All of them abiding by the Islamic dress code. Most Emirati males prefer a Kandura, which is an ankle-length white shirt woven from cotton. The Arabs were a serious looking bunch. Whoever this circle was, they meant business. They lined up, forming a walkway for Falisa and Papa Bear as they walked down the stairs of the jet. Falisa was in front, her hands sliding down the metal rails as she sashayed her way down to the concrete. Each of the Arabs bowed their heads as she went. Soon as she got on the ground, she was led to the rear of the Hummer limousine.

Papa Bear also got the royal treatment. Eye contact and bows, and then he was escorted into the rear of the same limousine. The interior was expensive, suede leather, crystal glasses, top shelf champagne, and elegant lighting. Falisa and Papa Bear rested in the rear of the stretch Hummer by themselves, still not knowing where they were going or who they were going to meet.

As the Hummer began to pull off, Papa Bear noticed a hand carved wooden box full of Cuban cigars. He lifted the top, removed one, and looked Falisa dead in her eyes. "I'm sure we're good now. I can feel it."

He then fired up the cigar, cupping his hand in front of the flames out of habit. When it was lit, he pressed a button on the center console and allowed the window to crack open enough to release the smoke.

Falisa didn't respond. She was tired and drained, and it was showing in her eyes. She had every reason to be exhausted; she had been through hell and back in the last twenty-four hours. Although she had been snatched from the belly of the beast each time, freedom is something that she has never taken for granted. The threat of capture several times back to back had taken a serious toll on her. She folded her arms across her chest and adjusted herself against the soft leather to find a comfortable spot to relax. Her eyes softly fluttered, until finally, they stayed closed.

To Papa Bear, she looked peaceful. He knew she needed the rest. It was more mental than physical for both of them. Papa Bear watched her chest slightly rising and falling. He sat the cigar in the ashtray and left it there, and for the next twenty minutes, he rode and thought. Amil popped in his head, and all he could do was smile to himself. He loved her like she was his own, and he was proud of her, in his own way. Finally, he took a deep breath and leaned his head back against the soft leather. He could feel the engine of the Hummer vibrating; the crunching underneath the tires was getting louder.

Papa Bear looked out the window and saw the Dubai Harbor against the backdrop of some of the world's tallest buildings, and he felt the power of this beautiful place. The looming skyscrapers seemed to be a symbol of the will and fortitude of the people, daring even the Persian Gulf to challenge them. The vivid scene was enough to make a smile appear on his lips.

Papa Bear was so deep in thought about his new surroundings, that he didn't notice that they had reached their destination until the car abruptly stopped inside a huge garage with white walls, high ceilings and bright lights. An Arab man with sharp eyes, dressed in a two piece suit opened the door. Papa Bear touched Falisa on her knee, just enough to wake her up.

She smiled at him, and then she noticed the man standing there with the door open. He reached for her hand and she gave it to him. Casually, he guided Falisa out until her feet were planted on solid ground. She stretched and yawned, then stood there until Papa Bear was out.

The man closed the limousine door behind him, and then in perfect English, he said, "Welcome to Dubai."

He turned and walked toward a door, motioning for them to follow him. Papa Bear hooked his arm underneath Falisa's arm, and they walked side by side, following him as he climbed three concrete steps that took them to a small, white nondescript door.

The Arab unlocked the small door and held it open for them. They stepped into a large beautifully decorated room. The ceiling was high, and in the shape of a dome, it looked to be made of glass. The furniture was luxurious, antique Italian sofas and chairs were strategically placed around the room, accented by classic Italian side tables.

Falisa walked around the room, studying the ornate wall coverings and intricate art pieces. She was in awe. Falisa had always prided herself on her exquisite taste, but this was beautiful beyond anything she could've imagined.

Papa Bear joined her. He was a simple man, used to simple things, so he found the room to be a bit overwhelming.

The Arab watched them, amused at their reactions. This was just one of the sitting rooms in the 57,000 square foot estate. He wondered if he would have to revive them after they experienced the rest of the property. "I'll show you to your sleeping quarters," he said calmly, and then he turned on his heels and glided across the white marble floor.

Falisa and Papa Bear followed closely behind him. When they reached the entryway, Falisa gasped. A massive three tiered six feet wide and six feet long chandelier hung from the forty foot ceiling, nestled between twin marble staircases with wrought iron bannisters. Falisa was in love. She stood and took in the beauty of the foyer until Papa Bear discreetly cleared his throat and touched her arm.

"I apologize," Falisa said, and smiled at the Arab.

They moved into another wide spacious room with high ceilings and beautiful crystal chandeliers. And through that room, they came face to face with black French doors trimmed in 24karat gold, which sparkled underneath the lighting.

The Arabian stepped forward and turned both doorknobs. With a slight flourish, he pushed the doors open, giving them a view of an all-white bedroom that was truly fit for a king and queen.

5

The bedroom was spectacular. As their feet sank into the plush white carpet, they felt as if they were walking on a cloud. The walls were covered by silk brocade winter white fabric, except for the east wall, which was floor to ceiling glass, and provided a magnificent view of the moon-lit gulf. Falisa walked over to the window, deep in thought. The view reminded her of the similar glass wall she had at the sanatorium. Sometimes she would look out at the water from her sitting room, and imagine the things she'd do, once she was free of those walls. Now, here she was, a world away. Safe, but still not secure.

Papa Bear pulled up behind her, wrapped his arms around her waist, and held her. He felt her body relax in his arms and his cheek rested against hers as they looked out at the water, the moon, the still night. No words were spoken, they just enjoyed the moment.

Falisa rubbed her hand the length of his forearm and she slowly turned around and faced him.

Just behind them, the Arab man bowed his head, stepped out of the bedroom and pulled both doors closed. When he left, Falisa relaxed and came out of her clothes. Their bed was a king-size with four huge marble posts and organza curtains. When they made their way to the bathroom, the layout was even more breathtaking. There was a huge walk-in shower surrounded by marble and smoked glass. The knobs were 24K gold.

Falisa took everything off in front of Papa Bear and she stood naked in front of him. She smiled, and then stepped into the shower, turned on the water and stood there waiting for him. Their eyes feasted on each other. Then, while Papa Bear watched the water beat against her body, he slowly began to take off his clothes. When he was naked, he stepped inside the shower with her.

Her arms went around his waist and she looked up at him, the hot water massaging them together. Papa Bear carefully laced his arms around her neck and placed his mouth on hers. Their kiss was soft and passionate, nearly breathtaking. Falisa's hard nipples pressed against Papa Bear's bare chest.

Papa Bear moved his hands from around her neck and let them travel north, past her collarbone, until he had two handfuls of her breasts. Bear held Falisa's breasts and massaged them gently, slowly flicking his thumbs across her swollen nipples.

She closed her eyes, relaxed under his huge rough hands. She traced small circles on the small of his back and allowed her nails to lightly rake his skin as the sensations from his tongue and hands caused her pussy muscles to contract. They never broke their kiss, tongues twirling in rhythm, taking in the taste, breath and feel of the other as the water mixed with their body heat steamed up the shower.

With little effort, Papa Bear slightly bent his knees and lifted Falisa up into his arms. She smiled and wrapped her legs around his waist. Her arms wrapped around his neck. They stared at each other as Papa Bear moved his thick, massive penis to the opening of her vagina and Falisa moved it into the tight wet spot where it belonged. She let out a soft moan when Papa Bear entered her. He was huge, and he filled every inch of her tunnel.

Still inside her, Papa Bear walked Falisa against the shower wall. He pushed up in her even further. She began winding her hips, working her pussy muscles. She was begging him with her eyes, and he delivered. He slow stroked her like he had been waiting for this moment all his life. They both seemed to savor each hard thrust. He bent his head slightly and took a nipple into his mouth as he picked up the pace.

Falisa's breathing grew heavier by the minute, until she found her eyes rolling to the back of her head. Papa Bear saw the white of her eyes and felt her entire body began to tremble under his. When she came, it was warm and thick and coated Papa Bear like the glaze on a donut. She reached up and wrapped her tiny fingers around the gold shower head. She wanted Papa Bear to beat it hard.

She locked her ankles behind his back and Papa Bear moved his dick all the way up in her, pounding with all his might, while she threw it to him as best she could. Finally, his face frowned and he came inside of her. Her rhythm slowed, but her chest continued to rise and fall heavily.

Gently, Papa Bear lowered her to the ground and proceeded to wash her body. When he was done, she returned the favor. After they showered, they hit the bed, falling asleep in each other's arms.

The following morning, three beautiful women awakened Falisa and Papa Bear. Their skin was honey-gold, outlined by a black over-garment called an Abaya. The first lady carried a gold platter with toothbrushes and toothpaste, a bottle of mouthwash, dental floss and face towels. The second lady, presented on her tray, his and hers yellow gold Rolexes with a face full of black diamonds. The third lady made them stand.

She pulled out a thin measuring tape and got both of their sizes, and then they were gone.

An hour later, Falisa was dressed in a long flowing dress with her head wrapped, in deference to the Islamic dress code.

Papa Bear told her she looked beautiful in anything, and that was that. He was dressed in pants, a cool linen shirt and expensive leather sandals.

A knock came from the door, and their host from the night before was back. He had an honest and trusting look. "Good morning." he said with a smile. "Ma'am... sir. Follow me, please."

He turned on his heels and led them through the mansion and into a private room with wooden bookcases and rows of books on each shelf. A beautiful Oriental rug covered the floor. There was a half circle couch on their left and a half circle one on their right, with a thick glass coffee table in the center.

"You may be seated. The Khabir family will be with you in just a moment.

They sat down as the man disappeared through the door. Falisa and Papa Bear locked their fingers together. The wait for the arrival of the Khabir family was really nerve wrecking. It was obvious to Falisa and Papa Bear that they were filthy rich, and well connected. But what they didn't know was how in the hell they were connected to Amil.

The door opened and a line of butlers came in, four of them to be exact, all well-dressed. Then another line of Arabian maids entered, four of them as well. They wore gray dresses with white cloth aprons. A beautiful woman with very intelligent looking eyes followed them. She had thin, soft-looking lips, and her body was covered from head to toe in a black abaya. Her husband came in behind her. His presence alone radiated power and respect. His head was covered, and he wore an ankle length kandura and sandals.

His name was Majid, and his wife was Sahir. They were

both in their late forties and one of the richest families in Dubai. Majid's facial structure was strong and chiseled, and he wore a neatly trimmed full beard. He introduced his wife first to Falisa and then to Papa Bear. They shook hands and gave each other hugs while keeping smiles on their faces.

The wife stood in front of Falisa, holding her face between her hands. As she stared into Falisa's eyes, she started to cry. Falisa didn't have a clue what the tears were for, but she would sure know in due time.

"Falisa," Sahir said in her softest voice. "We're so glad you could join us." Then she paused, kissed each of her cheeks, and said, "Your daughter is like our daughter. We owe her one hundred favors."

Together, the four of them found a seat on one of the huge circular sofas. Majid ordered water, lemonade, and food from the butlers and maids. Then he sat back and relaxed next to Papa Bear. Moments later, he opened his mouth. "Amil... You must love her."

Then he began his story about how they had met and bonded.

6

Seven years earlier, the Khabir family was one of the strongest and richest families in the city of Dubai, with a combined net worth of sixty billion dollars. They owned banks in the United Arab Emirates, and in New York, London and San Francisco, California, along with several other underground investments that were a secret, known only amongst the family. This morning, Majid and his youngest daughter, Jamillah, rode in the rear of a glossy black Mercedes Benz limousine that was bullet proof and driven by one of his top security guards. Majid's daughter had recently celebrated a birthday. She was thirteen now, and beautiful as can be. Jamillah's skin was smooth and soft, the color of honey with bright pretty eyes. Her hair was long, shiny and silky.

Today, Jamillah was going on a school trip with the rest of her class. When the limousine driver arrived at the Dubai Harbor, a yacht was waiting with the majority of her classmates already on board. Just beyond the yacht, the waters of the Persian Gulf were sparkling blue and the sun's rays danced across it in a waving rhythm. Majid stepped out the rear of the limousine and stood with his hand extended out for his daugh-

ter. He squatted in front of her, held her face between his hands
and kissed her forehead. Then he looked in her eyes.

They stared at each other for a long moment; he kissed her
lips, and without another word, they hugged and then she ran
toward the plank and on to the yacht. Majid and his bodyguard
went to the trunk and removed Jamillah's suitcases, and the
bodyguard carried them alone. Majid leaned against the
Mercedes Benz and watched his youngest daughter depart
from him for the first time in her life. When the yacht began to
move, the other families that were also sending their kids off,
began to frantically wave. Majid just stood there with a warm
smile on his face.

Jamillah came to the rail and waved at her father. She was
happy as could be. He stayed there waving and blowing kisses
until they couldn't see each other anymore. Majid's bodyguard
tapped him on his arm while he stood at the open rear door of
the limousine. Majid didn't flinch at all, he was in his own
thoughts. The idea of his daughter going off on a trip for two
days was eating at him.

In the rear of the limousine, Majid pulled out his mobile
phone and dialed a straight through number to his daughter,
Jamillah. She answered it on the third ring. They talked for a
few minutes, and that relieved many worries for him. He told
her to call if anything came up, and in exchange, he would ring
her phone every three hours to ensure that she was alright.

But she wasn't.

PAPA BEAR WATCHED Majid drop his head as if he couldn't go
any further with the story. The room fell completely silent, then
he raised his head. His eyes were moist, and they darted from
Falisa to Papa Bear. He took a deep breath and got a hold of
himself.

"Our daughter was kidnapped by a Somalian gang. They later sold her to some Colombian drug lords. Our precious child had been missing for seven whole years, when one day we get a call from your daughter, Amil, saying she has our daughter."

His eyes were getting tearier by the second. He straightened his head and eyes. Raised his shoulders.

"So your daughter was a prisoner back in Columbia?" Falisa said. She was horrified, because she knew what those women had endured, and she was proud when Amil freed everyone over there.

Falisa crossed her left leg over the right one. This entire situation had just turned real. Her eyes were on Majid, their pain radiated between the two of them like an electromagnetic field.

Sahir was next to Falisa. She took her hand, and with an understanding smile, she leaned in and pressed the side of her face against hers.

"Amil freed our daughter and brought her back to us."

Then Majid added, "Seven years later."

His Middle Eastern accent was thick and his English was perfect. They had given their child up for dead, and to have her back, made him the happiest man that walked the face of this earth. He turned to Papa Bear and politely placed his hand on his shoulder. "Amil also shared her story with us. She told me about your situation, and I want to let you know that you have our support for the rest of your days."

Again, the room fell silent. Majid snapped his fingers, and three minutes later, a maid came in with a bottle of 1953 Domaine Leroy Musigny Gran Cru wine. Then they brought four shiny wine cups made of gold. When everyone got their drink in their hand, Falisa asked, "So, what's next for us?"

"You can stay here in Dubai forever, if you like." Majid said.

"And what about Amil?" Papa Bear asked.

"We will work it out with the United States," he said, then added, "We have very good connections over there."

He stood up quickly and held his cup up. Papa Bear, Falisa and Sahir stood up also. They raised their cups and sipped. Everyone was quiet for a brief moment. The feeling was unusual. Papa Bear thought of it as a better position. On the other hand, Falisa thought of Amil as the best of the best. She looked at Sahir, stared in her eyes, still holding her wine cup. They'd experienced some of the same pain.

Sahir stared Falisa back in her eyes, then she began shaking her head side to side in a slow rhythm. "We would like to be Amil's godparents, with your consent."

"Amil is my heart," Falisa said. Her words came low, but strong. Her eyes drifted to Majid. He stood there, firm and solid, waiting for Falisa. "You definitely have my consent." She sipped from her cup. A smile appeared over her face, and then Falisa said, "I don't know how to thank you, but to say thank you."

Sahir moved closer to Falisa, wrapped her arms around her, and held her close like they were long lost sisters. "We would like for you to meet our daughter, Jamillah," she whispered softly.

Falisa smiled proudly. She looked towards Papa Bear and Majid; they were standing side by side, both of their faces displayed happiness and loyalty. That made Falisa feel even more comfortable. Still, she asked the question. "Where's Amil?"

7

S murf tried his best to readjust to normal life after January was murdered, but it was hard for him. Something like that would crush any man. He had watched her die, and was even hit himself, but his wounds weren't life threatening. This morning, he rode on the passenger side of a black Lincoln Town car with mid tint. Not too dark. Not too light. Behind the steering wheel was an older man, his personal driver and bodyguard. He was huge man like Papa Bear. His name was Frank; he stood an even six foot five and weighed close to three hundred, with wide shoulders and neck, and strong hands and powerful arms.

As he pushed the Lincoln through the early morning traffic, Smurf stared blankly out the window from his reclined seat, watching the passing cars as they finally entered the city of Augusta. He found the button, pressed it, and his seat came up to its normal position.

Frank glanced at him one quick time and put his eyes back on the road. "You good?" was all he asked.

Smurf opened the middle console, pulled out a pair of Gucci shades and placed them on his face. His dreads were longer and thicker now, and he wore them tied and bundled, leaving his handsome face exposed. Finally, he whispered, "No doubt." Then he was silent again.

Frank drove on, the Lincoln was smooth and the engine was quiet. Smurf hadn't been back home in a while, not since they'd buried his fiancé and Pig Man. But today, he was there. It wasn't long before Frank pulled into the entrance of a huge cemetery. Smurf looked out through his window, watching the sea of graves and tombstones. The sky was a crisp blue with thick slow moving clouds above. From behind his tinted shades, everything looked gray and cool. There was a line of cars, and a hearse about fifty yards away. Several people were packed underneath a blue tent. Smurf turned his head away, then looked at Frank. "Make this left coming up." he said in a calm and steady voice.

Frank was already on the brake, bringing the big Lincoln Town car to a slow creep as they turned left.

Smurf squinted and focused all his attention on the area where January was buried. He saw her mausoleum from nearly forty yards away.

"Pull over right here," he said. Frank pulled the Lincoln Town Car onto the right shoulder, bringing the two right side tires onto the grass and then he brought the car to a complete stop.

"Pop the trunk, give me a few minutes." Smurf said, as he hooked his fingers around the door latch and pulled it.

He pushed the door open and stepped out. The hot air rushed his face as he stood still for a brief moment in Louis Vuitton boat shoes, cargo shorts and a wife beater. A long platinum and diamond chain hung from his neck with a 24-karat medallion in the shape of a Smurf. He eased his way around the Lincoln to the partially opened trunk and pulled out two dozen red roses fixed up in a beautiful vase. He didn't bother to close the trunk. With the roses, he walked across the soft dirt and headed toward January's gravesite.

NEARLY SEVENTY YARDS across the graveyard, three undercover DEA agents unloaded a riding lawnmower from the rear of a dooly truck, pretending to be a family owned lawn care service. On each front door of the truck, there was a sign that read, Dunlap Lawncare & Treatment Family owned and operated since 1971. Two of the agents, both white of course, and medium built, dressed identically in khaki pants, boots and tan colored shirts with fake name patches over their right breast, carefully moved the John Deere mower to the ground. They turned it around and aimed the front end in the direction of where Smurf stood. Inside the headlights of the John Deer tractor, there were high tech voice recording devices that could hear and record sound up to one hundred yards away. But this was only a backup. Their main recording/listening devices were sitting on both sides of January's headstone.

The third undercover was in the rear of the Dooly, he was a blond guy with gray intelligent looking eyes. He was clean-shaven. No moustache. No beard. A strong structured face. He eased his headphones on his head and pressed a button on a small box in his hand. A small light turned green, it was the size of a match head tip and indicated a 'GO.' Then he heard Smurf's voice come through the earpiece loud and clear: *Your mother wouldn't let me come to the funeral. And you know that hurt me to my heart.*

Silence.

The agent waited and turned in his seat a little. He looked out the window, and noticed that one of his associates had hopped on the riding lawn mower and had slowly began to creep across the huge graveyard. The other agent was just for the hidden surveillance. He moved on feet, with a hidden camera inside a leaf blower.

I'll only be here in Augusta for a couple more days.

Silence again.

Then he heard Smurf breathing. Maybe he was trying to find the correct words to tell her. Then again, he could've been waiting for her to respond. Either or, he was quiet. Then he started again. *I hate that I put you in this position, Jan.*

Another pause.

But you can best believe, baby, the niggas that did this will be punished by any means necessary.

Smurf was taking his fiancé's death so hard, that he began to choke on his words. He actually sat down on the side of the concrete slab, removed his shades, and wiped his eyes with the back of his hand. He took another long deep breath and set the flowers on the ground next to him. He pulled his knees up, wrapped his arms around them, and sat quietly.

In the distance, he heard a blower, raised his head and scanned the cemetery. He saw the white guys as just plain workers. Undercover federal agents weren't on his mind by a long shot. Then he said, "I think I'll go to Paris and stay with Fly and Iris for a lil' while."

He pushed himself up off the ground and wiped the dust from his backside. Without another word, walked back toward his driver, Frank, and the Lincoln Town Car. Not realizing he'd just opened a new case for the Feds.

8

Smurf had long money, just as well as the rest of the family. Big money. Old money. Millionaire money; or whatever one chose to call it. Riding through downtown Augusta on the passenger side of the Lincoln Town Car, he was in deep thought. Passing by rows of shotgun A-Framed houses and junkies and prostitutes walking the streets, they pulled up to a stop light at 15th Street. To their left was a Pump & Shop gas station. The area was crawling with activity. Hustlers were grinding, and a couple of women in their early twenties were campaigning in small shorts and small tops with nice hair do's. Smurf spotted a familiar face and then told Frank to pull into the parking lot.

Frank turned on his left signal. A white Camry was coming toward them in the opposite lane. When the car passed by, he whipped the Lincoln Town Car into the parking lot. From Smurf's side window, he spied a high glossed Sports Coupe Lexus. It was white, with white interior, pretty chrome rims, and no tint on the window. The nose of the Lexus was facing a set of payphones. Smurf recognized the car and the face of the driver.

Frank parked in a slot facing the front glass of the Korean owned and operated store. Without a word, Smurf opened the door and stepped out. In this area, he stuck out like sore thumb. He closed the door and walked past the gas pumps and back toward the white Lexus. On the driver side, a dark chocolate female who didn't look a day older than twenty years old, sat fixing her lip-gloss in the rear view mirror. Her hair was nicely done, and her nails were long and manicured with fresh paint. When she looked up and saw Smurf, she paused, then she smiled and squirmed to open the door.

Smurf stepped back just enough to allow her some room to step out. When her feet hit the pavement, Smurf noticed she was wearing some cute low cut pink and white Air force Ones, tight fitting jean shorts, and a tight fitting top that outlined her round breasts. "Damn nigga, it's been a while." She said to him and reached out for a hug.

Smurf stepped into her arms and they embraced. He cracked a small smile and said into her ear, "I'm in town for a few days." Then he pulled back and took a long look at her.

Her name was Tia, and Smurf knew her from middle school. He also knew she came from a family of hustlers; the white Lexus was given to her as a gift from her younger brother. Now, with Smurf being bored, and after losing January, he saw Tia as something or someone to pass his time with. He asked her, "What you got planned for today?"

Tia gave Smurf a sexual look, her eyes seemed to say, *Whatever you want me to.* Instead, she hit him with a simple, "Nothing." She reached up and touched the end of his dreads hanging on the back of his neck. "I love them."

An hour later, Smurf had taken Tia to a hidden stash house just over the bridge in North Augusta. The house was a flat level made of red brick with storm glass windows, and sat on ten acres of private property in a secluded area, hidden behind a wall of pine trees and dense green bushes. He rode in the car with Tia, sitting on the passenger side, lost in thought, his mind on January. He still couldn't believe it. Then he thought about the idea of bringing Tia to one of the family's hidden stash houses.

When Tia pulled into the driveway and parked her Lexus, Smurf had a sudden change of heart. He looked in the rear view mirror and saw Frank's face right behind him in the Lincoln Town Car. That eased his mind a little. Then out of nowhere, he said, "It's been a change of plans." He faced her, but he still had his shades on, and she really couldn't see his eyes.

Her face turned sour and disappointed. "What? Why?" She sounded like she was about to cry. Then she put the gear shift in park and rubbed her hand across his thigh. "I won't disappoint you, I promise."

Smurf moved her hand and placed it back on her own thigh. Then he reached into his pocket and pulled out knot of hundred dollar bills. He handed her the money. "Buy you something nice," he said, and then he stepped out the car and walked to the Lincoln.

Smurf was coming unraveled, making decisions that weren't sound. When he got to the passenger side, Frank already had his door open for him. When he sat down and closed the door, Frank looked at him. The engine hummed quietly. No radio was playing, and the girl, Tia, was watching them in her rearview.

"You sure you're good?" Franklin asked.

Smurf took a deep breath. He felt like the walls were closing in on him. Then, in a slow deep drawl, he said, "Something don't feel right, Frank." His head fell back against the headrest.

Frank put the car in reverse. He did a U-turn and exited the driveway. Smurf closed his eyes. January was heavy on his mind and heart.

9

After Agent Paul Edgar found out that he'd been suckered and played like a piano, he was hard on the case. His main focus was Amil Walker, Falisa Walker, and their entire organization. Nothing like this had ever happened to the federal agent. Edgar figured that if anyone could get photos of his family and alter them to the point that they'd look real and official, they had to have a personal inside connect, and entirely too much pull.

Edgar had the green light to take this case as far as necessary in order to bring down their entire organization. At a federal building in downtown Miami, Agent Edgar sat inside a long square room at a polished wooden table. He was alone, and there were file folders stacked in a pile. He flipped open the first file with a photo of Timothy Timbo Walker attached with a paper clip; his name was on the front in black bold letters. He reached inside his top shirt pocket, removed his reading glasses, and eased them on his face. Then he opened the file. He scanned over the brief bio. Timbo had been in the drug game for years, the paperwork stated. He'd sold kilos of cocaine up and down the entire east coast, but no drugs were found during the raid of his Georgia home. Only weapons were recovered from inside the estate. He continued to read, his eyes carefully reading every word all the way down to the bottom of the page.

He flipped the page, read some more, and then he found out that Timbo's parents had been murdered and he was allowed to go to the funeral. The comments stated that men dressed up like women, in dresses with dark veils over their faces had surprised them. That was the last time Timothy Timbo Walker was seen by any federal agent.

Edgar took a long deep breath and sat back in his chair. *The deception and illusions have been going on for years,* he said to himself. *That's interesting, very, very interesting.*

Next, he flipped through a few 8x10 photos, some were in color, and others were in black and white. Most of them were of Timbo and Falisa when they were younger. Falisa was in a one-piece swimsuit, and Timbo was in swimming trunks. The water in the background was a beautiful blue; they were holding hands, walking side by side at Myrtle beach, South Carolina. They definitely looked happy together, no doubt about it.

The next photo was of the family. Timbo, Falisa, Fly and Amil were at Six Flags over Georgia. Amil was on Timbo's neck eating cotton candy with one hand and covering Timbo's left eye with her other hand. She looked happy, young, and innocent as can be. *Maybe she wasn't the one that called my phone,* he thought, while studying the photos. It would be hard to prove in trial. He put his hand underneath his chin and thought long and hard. There was an undercover DEA dead and no suspect in custody.

Edgar picked up the phone on the table next to the stack of files. He punched a button. One number, and the phone began to ring in his ear. After the third ring, someone answered from the other end. It was the director in Quantico. Edgar briefed him quickly. The director agreed with everything and gave

Edgar the green light, even if it was off the record. That alone made Edgar want to go harder.

When he got off the phone with his supervisor, he dialed a few more numbers and got in contact with some of his old street contacts and ex federal agents that never played by the rules. It was beyond time for this organization to be wiped out, even if it meant death. Agent Edgar smiled and sat back in his chair, his hands behind his head, lost in his own world. Now it was his turn, his own way, with no hang-ups, no negotiations, no pleas, no I'm sorry, or anything in that category.

For the rest of the day, and on into the night, Agent Edgar went through every file and every photo. He'd called every other agent who was on the case in the past, and collected anything concerning the Walker family since they'd started. Faxed paperwork began pouring in left and right. He wouldn't leave one rock unturned. Another agent came in, a long legged female with sandy red hair, green eyes and freckles. She wore a crisp white blouse and blue skirt that stopped just above her knees. Her name was Teresa Miles, and she was in her early forties and didn't look a day over twenty five.

She stood over agent Edgar with three more files and a box of recorded information from some audio surveillance. "You're gonna love this." She said and carefully placed everything on the table.

Edgar looked up at her; he flashed a half a grin. His eyes looked tired and drained. He reached up, patted her shoulder, and told her thank you. Then she was gone, just as quickly as she'd come.

Agent Edgar eased his elbow up on the table and propped his hands underneath his chin. Then he began searching through the new paper work that was stamped with bold red letters, *Confidential Information*. When he started flipping pages and reading the transcript of the recorded conversation, he was overwhelmed.

10

W hen Frank and Smurf got back to Atlanta, it was near midnight and Smurf was tired. In the last few months, he'd developed massive headaches off and on. His private doctor told him it was from stress, lack of rest, and paranoia since they'd been ambushed when he was shot, and his fiancé, January, was killed.

Frank pulled up to the entrance of Smurf's estate. This one was fairly new. He'd moved into this imposing six bedroom estate after the tragic accident. Frank pressed a button. His window came down and he punched in a four digit code on a mounted security pad. A red light flashed then it switched to green. Within seconds, the eight-foot iron fence blocking the driveway began to roll back, making an opening for the Lincoln Town Car. Frank eased off the brake and slowly rolled up the black top winding driveway. The halogen headlamps danced across the trees and evenly cut grass.

The driveway opened into one huge circle that was made of cobblestone. Frank pulled the Lincoln up the front door. The motion sensors were triggered and bright floodlights illuminated the entire front of the estate. He put the Lincoln in park then the front door of Smurf's house opened.

Another one of his bodyguards was standing in the threshold; he was huge also, and dressed in all black. His gun holster hung from his shoulder with the Beretta tucked inside. When he came down the short flight of stairs, two huge and well-trained German Shepherds came out behind him. They sat down in unison and looked directly up at him. Trained on his command. He walked up to them and patted both their heads. Then in low tone, he said to them, "Perimeter check."

Immediately, they stood up. One took off toward the east side of the estate, moving strong and steady across the lawn. The other one did the same, except he went west, and the flood lights made him look like a fierce Lion. Smurf liked his dogs, he felt protected with them, and even with his personal body-guards. They were trained killers, highly skilled with their hands. And as usual, Papa Bear had brought them in.

Frank closed the passenger door and pulled the Lincoln around the side of the house toward the four-car garage in the back. The other bodyguard that stood in front of Smurf was huge, a six-foot monster, weighing three hundred pounds of pure solid muscle. Smurf dapped him up. "What's good, gangsta?" They walked up the stairs and inside the house. The huge bodyguard stopped in the foyer. Turned around and locked the door.

Inside the living room, Smurf moved fast. He always walked straight through it. Easing across the marble floor as if he was gliding into the kitchen. The kitchen was HGTV worthy. Everything was stainless steel, with custom cherry wood cabinets and black marble surfaces. Smurf sat on a cushioned stool and rested his elbows on the marble countertop. He looked around, lost for words. This life was getting boring to him now. He had done everything there was to do in Atlanta, except for a couple of R&B females he had his eyes on.

Smurf got off the stool, went to the fridge, and pulled out a small tray of diced fruit that was covered with Saran Wrap. He moved the thin film, threw a piece of diced Mango in his mouth, and chewed quickly. After closing the fridge, he turned around and met Frank and the other guard, who went by the name, Bull. Frank carried a small cellphone in his hand and handed it straight to Smurf. He put it up to his ear with a surprised look.

"What up, brah?" Fly said.

Smurf's eyes went from Frank to Bull. They both were watching him cautiously.

"I'm alright, brah," he finally said. "Went down to Augusta today and visited Jan's grave."

Fly was silent for a minute, then he responded. "You need a vacation, brah. Why don't you come on over and visit me."

Smurf got another piece of fruit and tossed it in his mouth. Then he turned around and walked down a wide hallway that led to his spacious bedroom. He went through the door and said to Fly, "I actually thought about coming over there for real."

"You might as well. The Arabs fucking with us the long way. We just got a new Gulfstream G5 .Ain't even flew in the bitch yet. But I'll send the pilot to get you, if you want."

Smurf's bedroom was huge, with high vaulted ceilings and expensive lighting. Long floor-to-ceiling drapes in black suede covered the windows. Smurf eyed his bed; it was a huge king size. His mind was drifting, but he heard Fly loud and clear. "Damn brah... he said as he sat down on his recliner."

"Come on with the bullshit, Smurf." Fly said from the other end. "It's been two years, brah. Now it's time for you to come out that damn shell."

"I'm not in a shell, Fly."

"Alright... I'm coming to get you tomorrow."

"Naw, brah. Don't risk coming back to the states on the strength of me."

"Nigga, I been taking big risks. Just be ready. Charlie Brown airport in the P.M."

11

When Fly arrived in Atlanta the following evening, it was near dark. Sitting in a comfortable leather chair on the Gulfstream G5 jet, he wore a close cut full beard. Dressed in white linen pants, cool beige button up shirt, and ten-carat diamond rings resting in a mound of shiny platinum on each of his pinky fingers, he looked like a wealthy young playboy. His mouth was laced with veneers, white and expensive.

On the other side of the jet was a young Arab. He was in his early twenties, just like Fly, and he was Majid's cousin. He was the Arabian version of Fly. Both young men were very intelligent and very dangerous. His name was Abdul, he was short, maybe five six, and very handsome. His hair was black and oiled, and he wore it slicked toward the back. This was his first time in the United States, and he was already impressed before the plane even landed.

When the private jet finally came to a complete stop, Fly stood up and looked out the window. From his view, he didn't see a waiting car. There should've been a Lincoln Town Car or a yellow Ferrari. Fly turned, put his weight on his cane, and looked at his Arab partner, Abdul. "This nigga ain't here," he said in disbelief.

He turned back toward the window, scanned the airport, and didn't see a waiting car anywhere in sight. Fly took his phone out and speed-dialed Smurf's number. It rang several times, but there was no answer. He hung up and dialed the bodyguard, Frank's number. It rang. One. Two. Three. Four. Five. Six. Then an automated voicemail. Fly got worried then. He'd been with Smurf for too many years, and this was something that just didn't happen.

Fly hung up and called one of his other contacts in Atlanta to request a car to the Charlie Brown airport asap. Thirty minutes later, Fly and Abdul were in the backseat of a black Lincoln Town Car that was identical to the one Frank drove. Fly called Smurf's phone again while they drove. Again, no answer. Fly's heart was throbbing and his gut feeling wasn't positive at all. They rode on in silence. Fly reached down and unzipped the leather duffel bag that was between his legs. Inside was a mini arsenal of fully automatic handguns and something even more dangerous in the trunk.

Thirty minutes later, night had completely fallen and the driver had finally made it to Smurf's estate. At the gate, it looked lonely and deserted. The lights were out. Fly stepped out, walked up to the electronic key pad, punched in the code, and the gate began to roll back. Fly got back in the car, closed his door and they cruised up the winding driveway. The estate was hidden by trees and dense bushes. From the backseat, Fly watched and studied everything. Abdul sat quiet next to him, his eyes trained on the outside as well.

The driver continued on in silence. Another man was in the passenger seat. He was there for one purpose, and that was to kill whoever was the set target.

The Lincoln Town Car pulled up in front of the house. The driver put the car in park, but left it running. The guy in the front passenger seat stepped out and walked around to the trunk, which the driver had popped from inside. He raised opened it to reveal three fully automatic assault rifles wrapped in a brown checkered blanket. He lifted one of them. It smelled like fresh oil and was equipped with a hundred round drum and a retractable stock that made it a little longer than his arm. When he got it in his hand, he chambered one immediately.

Fly stepped out, followed by Abdul. The Arab took one of the other assault rifles. He was a gun specialist and knew everything there was to know about guns. He chambered one and quickly checked it. Fly walked up the steps, his gun in his hand. The Arab and the other guy was behind him. Fly pressed the illuminated doorbell about ten times straight, and still there was no answer. Fly knew something was definitely wrong for real. This wasn't Smurf. Not like this. Not answering the phone. Not answering the door. He knew he had guard dogs inside, but they were trained not to bark at intruders.

He took a deep breath, turned, and looked around. The Arab turned the brass doorknob and it opened a little. No alarm came on, and there were no signs of any dogs. Fly faced the front door, but the young Arab stepped inside the foyer first. He had his assault rifle ready and aimed; his finger fast on the trigger. The guy from the front seat went in next. They were moving like Navy Seals.

The inside of the house was pitch black and the infrared beams danced around the walls and made the home look like a disco. Fly came in last, and the first thing he did was call out Smurf's name.

There was no answer.

Fly took another deep breath. He was standing with his back against the wall. When he came off, he was walking like he didn't care what or who was around the next corner. The trio was ready. Fly had started sweating on his forehead; he wasn't expecting a situation like this. They got closer toward Smurf's great room. Fly was standing at the door, his ear close to it, trying to see if he could hear anything. To his surprise, he heard a voice that was low and far away.

Fly had the barrel of his Sig Sauer pressed against the door. He looked back at Abdul, and then his eyes shifted to the other guy. Fly nodded to them. He put the gun in his right hand, then wiped the sweat from his face with the end of his sleeve. With his free hand, he twisted the knob quietly. But before he pushed the door open, Abdul got down on one knee and took aim with the assault rifle. The other guy stepped to the side, away from any bullets that may come from the inside.

Fly got himself under control, then he stopped breathing and cracked the door open about half an inch. He allowed his right eye to peep through the small crack. What he saw, told him that something was horribly wrong. The bodyguard, Frank, was sitting in a double stuffed leather chair, his eyes wide with surprise. Last, but not least, there was a Chinese sword plunged through his chest and punching all the way through the back of the chair.

Then Smurf's voice came in an easy tone. "I'm just trying to live my life."

Fly pushed the door open further and he noticed Smurf standing at the long billiards table chalking up his pool cue and looking down his nose at the balls spread across the table. Fly walked all the way in. He dropped his hand and held his gun down low by his legs. Abdul followed close behind Fly, swinging the assault rifle from right-to-left.

In another chair on the opposite side of the room, the other bodyguard had met the same fate as the first one. Eyes open, mouth open and disgusting. Over by the huge fireplace, both

German Shepherds lay in small square area in front. Apparently, they'd been stabbed to death with the swords also.

Fly walked up to the billiards table. Smurf was on the opposite side, still chalking up his cue and looking at the table. Fly sat his gun down on a marble side table and asked Smurf, "What's wrong, brah?"

12

Smurf slowly looked up at Fly. He recognized him immediately. "Get yo' stick," he said calmly, as if he was not standing in the middle of a horror scene.

Fly walked over and removed a pretty wood-finished cue and turned back toward the table.

Smurf walked to the top of the table and raised his cue. The balls were already racked. He looked at Fly again. "These niggas the Feds, brah." was all he said, and then he bent slightly at the waist and carefully lined his stick up with the cue ball. With one powerful push, he slammed the cue ball into the pyramid of high and low balls and they scattered all over the table.

The smell of urine and feces permeated the air, the smell of death was palpable. Abdul and the other guy relaxed a little. They both lowered their assault rifles and stood on either side of Fly, staring at Smurf.

Fly leaned on the pool table, hands palm down on the edge. He looked at Smurf a long time. He was in some kind of daze or something, Fly figured. Then he asked, "What about the dogs? You paid good money for them, brah."

Smurf cut his eyes at Fly, and in the simplest tone of voice, he said, "Oh. They was undercover federal agents, too. You know the feds be having dogs, too. The he pushed his cue stick toward the cue ball, and carefully slammed it into the four ball. It was supposed to drop in the right side corner pocket, but it recoated off the velvet. Fly stood there briefly, just looking at Smurf. Then Smurf's eyes went to Fly. He shook his head in disgust because his shot didn't fall. Then he pointed at the table. "Yo shot." he told Fly.

Fly looked back, making eye contact with Abdul, and then the unknown associate. He addressed them both at the same time. "We gotta get their bodies wrapped up and make 'em disappear."

The other guy nodded and turned on his heels, pulling out his cellphone as he walked. Abdul walked over to the dead body of the man who was called Bull. He stood in front of him, grabbed the handle of the bloody sword. It was wedged all the way through. He raised his foot, put it on Bull's midsection, and yanked the long sword from his body. He dropped it on the floor next to the chair he was sitting in.

Fly saw that he was handling business, and turned toward the table. He positioned himself behind the cue ball and slammed it into a pile of balls. They sounded, smacked, and scattered. Then Fly moved over next to Smurf and said in a calm voice, "Do you realize that these are Papa Bear's people?"

Smurf looked at Fly, shrugged slightly, and moved around to the opposite side of the table. He exchanged the same calmness in his voice. "Well, he must be the Feds, too."

Fly paused. He looked at Smurf in disbelief. He knew he didn't say what he thought he heard. His face turned into a frown, cocking his head side to side. Then he slapped the pool cue against the side of the pool table so hard that four inches of the tip cracked and broke off. It flew over Smurf's head.

Smurf stared at him, his eyebrows bunched together, then

without warning, he reached around in the small of his back. His hand clutched the butt end of the handgun, but before he could get a chance to remove it, Abdul raised the assault rifle dead center of his chest. The infrared beam was on him. He yelled out in Arabic, "You'll die tonight."

Fly turned and looked at Abdul, then he put his hand on top of the barrel. He pushed it down, and then walked around to Smurf, stopped dead in front of him, and stared him square in his eyes. Smurf released the gun, and then he felt himself falling apart emotionally. He hugged Fly, and they held on to one another like long lost brothers. Fly patted Smurf on his back, and Smurf felt his tears pushing forward through his eyes.

Fly heard him sniffing and he pulled him tighter. The love was unexplainable between the two of them. Fly whispered in his ear, "I got to get you out of here."

Smurf didn't respond. In his mind, he saw January walking down the aisle in her beautiful wedding gown while he waited for her at the altar in his triple black tuxedo. Then that vision disappeared altogether, and that hurt him even more.

PARIS, FRANCE

13

T
he rain was coming down relentlessly, accompanied by harsh winds that had it blowing at a horizontal angle. Iris stood in her apartment window with the curtain drawn as the rain beat hard against the huge floor-to-ceiling window. The city of Paris was beautiful at night. Even through the rain, she could see the illuminated Eiffel Tower. Her view would be totally awesome on a dry summer night, far different from tonight. Like last night for instance, her view was perfect from her balcony. She would see the Louvre, Notre Dame Cathedral, and even the Arc de Triumph.

But now, here she was staring blankly out into the heavy rain. She was thinking about Fly, really scared and worried about him being back in the United States. He was supposed to be dead and cremated, but he was back in Georgia, of all states, like everything was official. She could only shake her head and turn on her heels at the same time. "Curtains please." she said aloud.

The voice recognition system acknowledged it and the curtains began to close automatically. The three-bedroom apartment that her and Fly shared was in the sixteenth

Arrondissement, and worth five point nine million dollars. The magnificent triplex came with a terrace and swimming pool. Their open area from the top floor offered them the best view of Paris from a three hundred and sixty degree angle. Iris walked bare feet across the thick soft carpet. "Damnit! Why won't he just change his fucking face?" she asked herself as she walked toward the couch. She was aggravated.

She sat down on the sofa and looked around at the expensive paintings on every wall around the high ceilinged and spacious living room. It was two o'clock in the morning, and Iris was lonely as hell. While sitting with her feet tucked underneath her, she stared at the huge wall portrait of Hawk and Timbo. The same painting that they'd taken from Hawk's mansion in the Hamptons. Her eyes focused long and hard, to the point that a frown came across her face. She hated it, but Fly loved it, and just because he loved it and looked at it as a trophy, she respected it.

She was up and on her feet again. There was a cordless phone sitting inside the charger. She went to it, picked it up and looked at it, but there wasn't anybody to call, except Fly. She couldn't call him, because in their last conversation, he said he would call her when he landed in Paris. That was two days ago, and to her, it had been two days too long. Now, following her gut feeling, she picked up where she started and punched in his number and put the phone to her ear. It rang once and went straight to voicemail. Iris' stomach flipped in a knot. She hung up then dialed it again. Same response, straight to voicemail. She took a deep breath and sucked her teeth as she dropped the phone back into the charging slot. She folded her arms cross her chest, then turned and walked down a narrow hallway and through a wide spacious sitting area with a glass roof. The rain was still coming down relentlessly.

When she stepped inside the huge-spacious bedroom, she went straight to the his and hers walk-in closet. Iris stepped into a pair of jeans and quickly pulled a thin sweater over her head. There was Louis Vuitton luggage stacked to her left behind her army of high heels. She grabbed a suitcase and pulled it to the middle of the closet floor. She popped the gold button and opened it. Her mind was somewhere else, mainly on Fly. She couldn't rest unless she found out where he was.

She began pushing a few pieces of clothes inside the suitcase, and then she closed it. Flipped off the closet light, grabbed the suitcase by the handle and backed her way out of the closet. In her bedroom, she walked to the chest of drawers and pulled one of the top drawers open. Inside was a fake passport with her photo, but a different name and date of birth. She was definitely on her way to the United States.

Ten minutes later, she had everything she needed. She went to her bedroom door, twisted the knob, and opened it. There, she stopped in her tracks; her heart felt like it had stopped completely. Fly was standing just on the other side of the door, and Smurf was next to him. She dropped everything she had and leapt into his arms with pure excitement and joy. Her arms went around his neck and she smiled.

She looked over his shoulders at Smurf, who was smiling at her like crazy. She let Fly go and hugged him next. He wrapped his arms around her waist. "Hey." She said to him, happy and relieved.

She stepped back and looked him up and down. He looked good, but in his eyes, she could see that something was worrying him. Instantly, she asked him. "What's wrong, Smurf? You don't look good."

Smurf flashed a smile, masking his feelings. He grabbed both of her hands, looked her straight in her eyes, and then suddenly he looked over at Fly. Fly slowly shook his head from side to side, telling him it wasn't a good time to tell her. Then he shifted his eyes back to Iris. "Maybe later." He quickly changed the subject. "You look beautiful."

She rolled her eyes, pulled her hand from his and headed toward the kitchen. "I'll cook." She said and walked around the next corner until she faded from their sight.

Smurf looked at Fly, and Fly shrugged and walked into his bedroom. Smurf followed behind him and closed the door. Fly took off his pants, laid them across the leather Ottoman that was at the foot of the bed. Then he carefully removed his prosthesis and left it standing there.

Smurf went to the window and slightly parted the curtain. The rain was still coming down hard and beating across the window. He saw Fly on the bed looking at him from the window's reflection. "I fucked up, brah?" he asked Fly while looking at him through the glass.

Fly was fluffing up his pillows and getting comfortable. He said, "Yes, you know you fucked up."

Smurf knew he'd fucked up, and now he was trying to figure out a way to break the news to him. He took a deep breath and faced Fly, then he moved over toward the bed and stopped just at the foot, his eyes on Fly. "What I need to do?" he asked in a strong and confident voice.

Fly exchanged the same look. "We gonna have to call a family meeting." Fly said, but he really wanted to tell him that he'd lost his mind and that he needed to be evaluated by a psychiatrist. He would definitely suggest it once the entire family was together. Then he thought back to what Smurf said back at the estate in Atlanta. *What about the dogs? Oh, they were undercover Federal agents, too.*

The silence hung between the two of them for nearly ten minutes.

14

Iris was sitting at the stone counter topped kitchen breakfast bar. On the opposite side of her was an older lady who they'd hired as their cook and housekeeper. The lady was in her mid-fifties, chubby, and stood five-three. She started setting the table for them. Iris watched her place the fine china and crystal glasses, while she nursed a hot cup of steaming coffee. From behind her, Smurf came in. She looked behind him to see if Fly was coming up in the rear, but he wasn't.

Smurf put his arm around her neck, gave her a quick and friendly hug, and slid on the stool next to her. He eased his elbows up on the counter top, and looked over at Iris.

She turned to him. "What's going on?"

Smurf took a long drawn out deep breath, and finally said, "I fucked up, Iris."

Her eyes were on him. His were on the cook standing over the stove about to scramble some eggs. Then he went on. "I killed my bodyguards. Both of them."

Iris didn't look surprised. She heard his words and processed them quickly. She told the cook to bring her a glass of orange juice,. Then she looked at Smurf. "You want something to drink?" she asked him.

Smurf shook his head. His eyes met Iris' eyes and they studied each other for a few seconds. The lady brought Iris a half filled glass of orange juice. Iris took a swallow. She looked back to Smurf and said, "So I got to call Papa."

"I figured you was gonna say that." Smurf said and shook his head slowly.

NEARLY AN HOUR LATER, the cook had set the breakfast table for three. Fly was comfortable. In front of him was a plate with two egg omelets, turkey bacon and a half grapefruit. Next to him, Iris sat quietly, only listening while Smurf explained the story. At least his side, anyway. But hell, there wasn't anyone to say otherwise, but Papa Bear.

Fly turned and looked Smurf dead in his eyes. He folded a piece of the turkey bacon and stuffed it in his mouth, and then he let out a small laugh and said, "Well, I came to my conclusion."

"Honestly," Smurf turned up a glass of orange juice, but he never took his eyes away from Fly. When he sat the glass back down, he asked him, "What's your conclusion?" His eyes went from Fly to Iris, back and forth. Silence hung in the air for a moment. Smurf was waiting on a response.

"You haven't been right since January and Pig Man left us."

Iris added, "And you know we want the best for you, Smurf. I'll explain everything to Falisa and Papa. I'm sure everything will be fine."

Smurf looked around. He wasn't nervous, but his eyes were giving off something else. An unsure type of vibe that Fly hadn't ever gotten from him since they'd known each other. The kitchen was silent yet again. Smurf picked up his fork and cut into his omelet, stabbed the small piece and picked it up and stuffed it inside his mouth. He chewed, swallowed, and thought about his actions in the last few months. He looked up at Fly, and out of the blue, he said, "The Arab dude drawed down on me. He must not know me?"

"You were ready to draw on me, Smurf." Fly said. "Hell, I don't even know if I know you."

"Fly, you know me."

"I know, Smurf. And the Smurf I know wouldn't have ever attempted to draw down at me."

Iris was listening and looking from one to the other. She didn't know about that part, and just that alone made her realize that something was indeed wrong with Smurf, and soon, they'd figure it out.

15

When agent Paul Edgar landed in Virginia, there was a dark green Taurus with tinted windows waiting for him. Two federal agents were inside the car. A white female was in the driver seat, and an older white man was in the passenger seat. Edgar walked with a briefcase gripped in his hand; he wore a dark two-piece suit, a white shirt and a striped tie. When he got to the Taurus, he went straight to the rear passenger door, climbed inside, and pulled the door closed. He tapped the female agent on her shoulder and addressed her by her first name. "Morning, Carol."

Then he touched the older guy on his shoulder. "Stan, how you doing?"

The Taurus was already running. Carol put the selector in drive and eased out of the airport parking area. They nearly said good morning to him at the same time. Stan adjusted his rearview mirror after flipping down his visor. His eyes found Edgar's eyes and he said. "It's been a change of plans."

"A change of plans like what?" Edgar asked. His tone changed a little. He definitely didn't want to hear that.

Stan had been in the government for over twenty years. He was one of the big wigs with the DEA. He stared at Edgar again through the mirror while Carol got out into traffic. Stan took a deep breath and finally said, "The federal government is off the Walker family case.

Edgar's face turned into a frown and he rubbed his hand over it in disbelief. "Why Stan? I don't understand. I got everything under control. I know about their hideout in Paris, and I got enough valuable information to send the whole family to prison, high max at that, for the rest of their lives."

"You got to understand, Edgar. We lost one of ours. McElroy was one of our best undercover agents, and she was killed, murdered by these people. There was an untraceable, odorless poison found in her blood that is impossible to obtain here in the States, so that alone tells us that they have connections out of the country. The Colombian cartels are backing them, and it's costing us too much money to apprehend them. The one key witness we had ready to testify, was murdered along with the rest of his family." His eyes fixed straight on Edgar from the mirror. He turned in the front seat sideways, now looking Agent Edgar directly in his eyes. He asked him, "Didn't the girl call your phone and tell you this herself?"

Edgar nodded, taking everything in, word for word. Then he shook his head. Edgar wanted this case and he wanted it bad. These people had played on his intelligence, and that was the utmost disrespect, considering he was a government official and worked for the DEA. Agent Edgar asked, "Whose decision?"

"It's bigger than us. The call is coming from up top, and from here on, this case is officially closed and off the record. Our people have gotten restless."

Edgar looked away from Stan and focused his stare on the passing trees. The scenery was boring to him, and that didn't make the situation any better. When he finally looked back at Stan, he asked, "So what do we do now?"

Stan turned back around and looked straight ahead out the front window. "You're only on a need to know basis here, Edgar. But I think you've been affected by these people, so you deserve to know what's going on." He got silent again and glanced over at the driver. She was listening, but her head and eyes were straightforward. When Stan looked back in the mirror, he said calmly, "We're sending in a team. Special Forces, some of the best trained killers that ever worked for our government, and we kill them, one by one, from the mother on down to the children.

Edgar didn't expect to hear that. That last sentence made his flesh crawl. He was looking out the window again. There was a sea of brown fields passing quickly, and it looked as if it stretched for miles and miles.

"And what we're gonna need from you, is to provide us with any and all information you have pertaining to their whereabouts that will lead us straight to them. Trust me on this, Edgar. We'll all sleep better once this is over."

Edgar sat quiet as they rode up the long stretch of highway. His mind was on something else, which was also involved with the case. *These people are strong*, he thought. *They had pictures of my kids and wife, and my parents, but it was all a hoax.* That alone made him agree with the idea of taking them out.

He lifted the briefcase and sat it on his lap with the open end facing him. Edgar clicked the brass locks and opened the top. He pulled out four thick manila files that were filled with several photos, tape recordings and information on each of the family members. He handed everything over to Stan in the front seat.

Stan thumbed through it all as they rode. The car slowly pulled to the side of the road, nearly came to a stop until she did a U-turn and took the Taurus back toward the way that they just came.

"I thought we were headed to Quantico." Edgar said.

"I want you to take a vacation, Paul. Take your family and relax. You deserve it." Stan responded.

"Like hell, Stan." Edgar's eyebrows bunched together. "You wanna know what I deserve, damnit! I need this case, I need it, Stan. You got to keep me on."

The car continued in the opposite direction, heading right back toward the airport where they'd picked him up. The talking stopped once again. Edgar was waiting on a response. Instead, Stan flipped the visor up, so that Edgar was no longer in his reflection.

Edgar sat up, his hands on each of the headrests. "So you don't believe in me?"

"It's not that I don't believe in you, Paul. It's just out of my hands now." Stan pulled out a pack of Marlboro cigarettes, thumped one from the bottom of the pack. He eased it between his lips and lit the cancer stick. Before the smoke could start circulating inside the car, he pressed a button and rolled his window down.

Now, with the wind blowing through Edgar's hair, he finally decided to give up. The hope was gone just that fast. Now the airport was coming into his sight again. Finally, he laid his head back against the seat, took a deep breath, and rode silently all the way back to the airport.

16

In Dubai, the billionaire Khabir family had furnished Falisa and Papa Bear with a brand new mansion, and in the Emirates the estates were huge and worth millions of U.S dollars. Theirs was located in the Emirate Hills Community, which boasts the world class Montgomery Championship golf course. Their villa was over 10,000 square feet, built up on a strong frame, and equipped with security monitors from every angle. Inside, there were eight bedrooms, ten baths, a two-story rotunda, and two huge kitchens. A study, library, home theater, gym, maid's quarters, were included, and to top it off, a subterranean eight car garage filled with nothing but exotic foreign cars.

Falisa was back to normal for a minute. She was lying in bed in her master suite, propped up against some double stuffed pillows. Her bed was comfortable, and even more relaxing. The atmosphere made her feel like she was on a private island. She flipped through the channels from the remote, and nearly every channel she went through they were speaking Arabic. Falisa got up and eased her feet inside a pair of bedroom slippers, and then she draped herself in a silk robe over her nightgown.

For some reason, she was bored. She walked over to the huge wooden double doors, turned the knob and walked out into the wide and spacious marble corridor. This house was much bigger than her old all white mansion back in Miami. Right outside her door, there were two Arabian men in khaki pants, black boots and fitted tee shirts tucked neatly inside their pants. Each of them carried side arms in leather holsters. Falisa nodded at them and kept it moving down the corridor. She opened a door on the left that took her to the study.

Papa Bear was inside, sitting at a huge mahogany desk in front of a computer. He looked up at Falisa when she entered the study. The scent of fresh flowers enveloped her. Standing next to Papa Bear was another Arabian man, slightly bent at the waist and staring at the computer along with Papa Bear.

Papa Bear stood up, and the Arab took his seat immediately. He walked around the desk to Falisa and stood in front of her. She looked up at him, fixed her mouth for a kiss and Papa leaned down and gave her one.

"What you up to?" He asked her and slipped his hands around her waist. Now looking in her eyes, he noticed that she was worried about something.

"I don't like when Amil goes missing, that's all."

Papa Bear kissed her forehead, smiled, and pulled her close to him. Her arms went around him. She felt so relaxed and comfortable in his arms.

"Amil is all right," he said, then after a pause, he went on. "And I'm sure of that, because there's been a family sit down called for tomorrow, and everyone must be there."

Falisa's face turned still and expressionless, her bright eyes looking up into his. "Who's the situation with?"

"Iris called Amil, Amil called me and—"

"You spoke with her?" Falisa interrupted him

Papa Bear stood there. The look in his eyes was his only response. She caught on quickly, and out of respect, she politely said, "I'm sorry."

"When Amil called me, she said there was a situation with Smurf."

"So where and when is the meeting?"

"One of two places," he said. "Here or either Paris. Now you got the final decision.

Falisa's eyes were on him. She was damn good at reading people, especially the ones that were close to her, but Papa Bear kept a straight face. She turned away from him and went toward the door.

Papa Bear moved behind her. She went through the door and stopped just outside it. Papa Bear pulled the door closed and stood there next to her. She looked up at him. "We're safe here in Dubai, but if we bring everyone here, that could spell trouble," she said. "We don't know what the feds know, and furthermore, who they're following."

"Okay, the states are off limits. So that leaves Paris, I assume."

Falisa paused. She was in thinking mode for a moment. Her wheels were spinning like no other. Then she said, "What if they know about Paris? For instance, they may be watching Fly and Iris right now. They may be the bait, but we're the sharks they want for the big catch. We know how the Feds play baby, by no rules."

"...So we'll bring everybody here." Papa Bear said and grabbed her hand. They walked down the corridor, headed straight for their bedroom. The two Arab guards were still there, looking straight ahead. Dead serious.

Falisa went through the door first, and Papa Bear followed behind her and closed the door. Falisa moved across the spacious floor and over to the high-glossed mahogany dresser.

There was a cushioned stool in front of it. She sat down and looked at her reflection in the mirror.

Papa Bear walked up behind her. He put a hand on each of her shoulders and massaged her lightly. She smiled and relaxed under his touch.

Falisa reached over her shoulder and placed her hand on top of his. "Are you sure you're comfortable with this decision?" she asked him.

"Dubai is our safe haven. Nobody knows we're here. We should be able to sneak the family in and get the situation under control."

Falisa sat quietly for a moment. She was thinking again. Fly was on her mind, along with Smurf and Iris. She finally said, "Fly is supposed to be dead, and I swear I don't like him going country to country like everything is official. You and I both know if Fly and Smurf come over here together, they'll be in all type of shit."

Papa Bear smiled, then leaned down and kissed her softly on her lips. "We on vacation as of now, we resting and relaxing, baby." He whispered in her ear, "After this, I would like to marry you, baby."

Falisa's eyes found his in the mirror. They stared at each other long and hard. Neither of them blinked, just staring so hard that they seemed to be looking into each other hearts and soul. Falisa heart was fluttering. She bit down on her bottom lip and then her face turned into a smile. "Under one condition," she said.

"I'm listening."

"I want to retire a billionaire," she said with a shrug. "Just to say I was the first bitch to ever do it from the streets."

Papa Bear finally breathed. Then he said, "Your wish is my command."

17

One of the gifts that Amil received from the Khabir family was her own private jet. It was a Gulfstream, and she sported it just like she was pulling up in front of an audience in a Maybach. When her jet landed in Dubai, the pilot pulled in front of a hanger until the plane finally came to a halt.

The huge doors on the hanger came open, then a convoy of SUVs came out, starting with huge black on black Hummer with tinted windows and huge knobby tires and thick grille guards covering the front. It muscled its way out, the two back windows came down, and a high caliber machine gun came out of each window, aimed and ready. The men behind the machine guns were nothing more than trained killers that spoke no English and wore their faces covered. The driver pulled past the Gulfstream and the stairs from the jet slowly came down. The Hummer in the front blocked off the steps.

The second Hummer, identical to the first one, came out the same way, except this one pulled up to the stairs and made a left, the nose pointing east, the machine guns emerging from the rear windows. What they were doing was blocking off the stairs, covering it from all directions. The last Hummer pulled up, the right rear door was ajar as the Hummer stopped inches from the jet.

An Arab man stepped out, dressed in a two-piece khaki-military style uniform, black boots. His face and head wrapped up in black, his eyes and nose visible and he carried a military issued assault rifle that wasn't used for a fashion statement whatsoever.

From the opening of the Gulfstream, two men came down the stairs first, both of them well dressed and standing over six feet tall. It was hard to tell if they were Middle Eastern or Colombian. Either way, they were black and very mean looking.

Next came Amil, covered from head to toe in a comfortable black abaya. She came down the stairs gracefully, allowing he tip of her fingers to trace along the metal railing. When she reached the bottom, she was carefully guided straight to the back seat of the waiting Hummer. Inside, she was with her bodyguards. The air conditioner blew softly.

Amil had the window seat, but there was a small wooden tabletop in front of her with a laptop computer on it. Amil looked out the window. In a distance, there were more private jets, lined up and parked. Her eyes scanned a little bit further, but nothing looked out of place. She turned on the computer in front of her. The screen illuminated instantly, and there was a small smiley face icon bouncing around from corner to corner.

Amil pressed a few keys and her private estate popped up on the screen, the second gift from the Khabir family. Amil was her own surveillance technician. She hit a couple of keys and the cameras zoomed in on the palm trees that surrounded the pool in the backyard. Her villa was worth well over twenty five million, and forty five thousand square feet. She tapped another key, and one at a time, all ten bedrooms popped up in a row and in color. Her housekeeper, an older Chinese woman was changing the linen in one of the bedrooms. Amil nodded her head at that.

The convoy of Hummers began to move and her eyes immediately shifted toward the window. There wasn't anything out there, she just looked out of habit. Her eyes went back to the computer screen. Everything around her living quarters looked secure and peaceful. Amil had every reason to be cautious now. She knew the Feds were thirsty, and smart, and they had patience. Her mother had killed an undercover federal agent. They were definitely mad at that. Amil knew they were growing impatient, she could feel it, but she couldn't put a finger on their next move yet.

The Hummers were moving across the parking lot like a straight line of Army tanks that were getting in position for war. It was early in the morning; the sun was rising quickly in the distance. When the Hummers picked up speed, the huge knobby tires left a trail of dust behind. No more than forty-five minutes later, the convoy was pulling into her compound. The villa was beautiful and surrounded by pure elegance. Amil admired her Dubai living quarters, even though she still had a spot in Colombia, another hide out estate in Cuba, and another one in Colorado, deep in the mountains.

Her movement was strong, and she was backed by her own personal Colombian cartel. She was still getting money from shipments of cocaine, and even more, she was all the way plugged in with the Arabs. They treated her like their very own daughter, and even gave her options to invest in a private oil field that would benefit her and the twin daughters of the Khabir family.

The three Hummers pulled around the rear of the compound. The one Amil was in pulled drove directly into one of the garage bays. The door came back down. The engine of the Hummer vibrated off the concrete wall. Amil waited for one of her bodyguards to come around and open her door.

She stepped down, holding the hand of one of the guards until she was safely out. The garage area alone was capable of holding at least twenty automobiles. She had them filled with everything from bulletproof Bentleys to foreign sports cars of all colors. Amil was clearly the head of the Throne now and calling all the shots, until Falisa felt that it wasn't going right.

When she got inside her home, her staff was there, the cooks, the mechanic for the cars and the housekeepers. She greeted everyone, kept it moving toward her huge master bedroom, and locked herself inside. In the privacy of her room, she unwrapped herself and took all of her clothing off. Her bed was sitting high off the floor, made of handcrafted wood and gold. The mattress was thick and wider than a king size. The doors to her balcony were wide open, giving her a magnificent view of the sea. Amil fell across her bed, dressed in a black lace bra and panties. A light wind blew across her skin.

She picked up her phone and dialed a number. Falisa's voice came across the line, and a smile spread across her face. "Good morning, Mother." she said cheerfully. Amil turned over on her back and stared up at the cathedral ceiling.

"Good morning. Where are you?"

"I'm here in the Emirates, just got in from Colorado. We'll all meet here this evening. Dinner party on me."

"Another one of your great surprises, I assume."

"Just laying out the pink print, Mother." She smiled. Amil liked the sound of that. Moving forward, the pink print was what she would say when she referred to her plans. Everything was coming together for her, and now she wanted to share it with her family.

18

Later that same evening, Amil was dressed in a fancy dress that out lined every curve of her body. She wore expensive black diamonds in each of her earlobes, a huge black diamond on her right hand. Open toed high heels made of black suede completed her outfit, and she smelled like a million bucks. Standing outside on the terrace of her bedroom, she enjoyed the breeze from the ocean and listening to the water crash against the rocks. Her view was stunning; in the distance, she could see the lights of a passing yacht.

Amil rubbed her hand along the railing that ran across the top of the low concrete wall. She was lost in thought; her mind was on her vision. She'd had tons of cocaine in Colombia, but as of now, she didn't have a customs connect. Not yet anyway, and it was slowing down her progress. The situation with the Feds wasn't helping. She had made a direct call straight to Agent Edgar. That was another mistake, but it was for a good purpose. Her mother was alive and free, and so was everyone else.

"Hey." A soft voice whispered from behind her.

Amil turned around. Jamillah was standing there; she was

strikingly beautiful. This evening, she wasn't wearing an abaya. Instead, she was dressed up in an evening gown. Her hair was black and silken, bone straight. Her body wasn't curved like Amil's, but she definitely pretty and petite. Amil wasn't expecting to see her today, even though it was good for them to see each other. Jamillah was the daughter that Amil had freed from the Colombians, and since that day, they were like distant sisters.

Amil moved over towards her and they hugged each other and slightly rocked side-to-side. "Hey girl," Amil said to her and pulled away but continued to hold hands.

They smiled at each other, and then, Jamillah said, "I got everything in place that you asked for. My sister, Khamillah, has a couple of friends at Yale University and Princeton."

"And they can handle that business, correct?" she asked seriously.

Jamillah was loyal to Amil, that part was clearly understood. She stared Amil straight in her eyes, her hands still gripped with hers. "I owe my life to you, Amil. And everything I say is bonded."

Amil squeezed her hands and kissed both of her cheeks. "Thank you." She released her hands and moved back inside her bedroom. Jamillah followed behind her. "Let's go greet the family." Amil told her.

Downstairs, the front of the estate was filling up with limousines. Three of them to be exact. Armed Arab men were standing around in khaki suits, their heads wrapped in black silk turbans. The first limousine was parked at the front door.

One of the Arabian bodyguards opened the rear door. Falisa stepped out first. Her black patent leather heels hit the paved flat top. She was dressed in a fitted black sheath, which clung to her waist and hips. Falisa had a powerful aura about herself. She just had that look, and over the years, she'd gotten better and better at showing it off.

Papa Bear came out behind her. He was dressed in a triple black tuxedo, black dress shoes, and his stature just as powerful. Papa Bear looked around, his sharp eyes scanning the many different armed guards that were spread around the estate as far as he could see. Security was looking good, and he would congratulate Amil and the Arabs for that.

The next limousine behind theirs was a white Mercedes with dark tint and bulletproof from the nose to the tail. One of the Arabian bodyguards walked up to the rear door and opened it. Majid stepped out, covered in an all-black kandura and a head wrap. He turned around immediately, and reached his hand out toward the door. His wife, Sahir, took his hand and exited the car. Her head and face were wrapped and she was covered in an abaya. Four more guards immediately covered them. They made a half circle around them and ushered the four of them toward the front entrance.

The last limousine moved up toward the entrance just as the other two were moving on around the circular driveway. Amil went to the rear door herself and opened it. The interior lights highlighted Fly's face. He looked at her from behind a pair of Dior Homme shades he'd had special ordered in Paris. He smiled at his little sister, turned and faced her. He put his cane out the door first and then he came out in a triple black tuxedo. They embraced, held one another for a brief moment. Fly kissed her cheek and let her go.

"Good to see you." she said to him.

"Good to see you, too."

Then Iris came out the limousine. She was in an evening gown, heels and she wore a string of diamonds around her neck.

She hugged Amil immediately, and they held on to one another for nearly three whole minutes. They separated, and then the man of the hour stepped out. Smurf was also dressed in a triple black tuxedo, black silk shirt underneath his jacket, with his dreads clean and pulled to the back in a ball. He looked at Amil and smiled.

Amil walked up and gave him a hug. She felt sorry for Smurf, but she was confident that he would be fine.

No more than ten minutes later, they were inside one of the dining rooms. This was the biggest one, with a long oval shaped marbled top table. The table was big enough for eighteen people, including a person at each end. Each setting had three glasses and more than enough silverware. Champagne flutes and whisky tumblers completed the setting.

The caterers and housekeepers were all related to the Khabir family, and they already had a few things laid out on the table, including Gotham steak and Colorado Lamb chops. There were three different types of rice, and tender goat meat.

Everyone found their places; there were nametags in each of the high back cushions seats indicating where each person would sit. For the first time amongst this family, Amil took the seat at the head of the table, and Jamillah, the daughter of the Khabir family took the seat at the other end. Her mother, Sahir, sat on one side of her and her father, Majid, was on the other side. Papa Bear sat next to Amil on her left and Falisa was on her right.

Well dressed maids came out with more food, some of the best dishes that money could buy. After ten minutes of chatter, the room got quiet when Amil tapped a fork against a crystal glass. Everyone focused their attention on her. Her eyes went directly to Smurf. She looked away from him, and then looked at Papa Bear. Amil smiled. He nodded and smiled back. Then her eyes went to everyone around the table, one person at time.

She cleared her throat. "First of all, I wanna thank each of you for coming out this evening."

Around the table, everyone returned the greeting.

Amil then slid her chair backwards and stood up. She went to the right side of the table, bypassing Falisa and Iris, and she stood behind Smurf and put her hands on each of his shoulders. Smurf sat patiently, he felt comfortable with Amil standing behind him. "For those of you that don't know, this is Smurf, my brother. Not by blood, but by loyalty. He's had a situation in the states and killed two of the family bodyguards."

Immediately, Papa Bear's eyes turned to slits. He froze and stared at Smurf. This was all new to him. *Family bodyguards?* He asked himself. *Not my people. Couldn't be.* Then Papa Bear asked, "Who we talking about?"

Smurf didn't panic; he knew how Papa Bear was about team players and definitely his personal people. He said, "Bull and Frank."

Papa Bear and Smurf stared into each other's eyes for nearly a whole minute. Silence hung in the air. Then Smurf said, "They were undercover agents, Papa."

Papa Bear shook his head. He knew good and damn well they were clean and legit. Clearly, something was wrong with Smurf. "And what made you think my people were undercover agents?" he asked.

Amil was still standing directly behind Smurf. She waited for him to answer Papa Bear's question, but he didn't. He couldn't respond, but instead, Amil finally said, "They weren't actually undercover agents, but they did testify years ago in a federal trial on some people out of Chicago, Papa. When I did the background check, that's what came up."

"So you ordered the hit?" Falisa asked.

Amil shrugged, then she smiled and said, "Just showing y'all who's on point and who's not." She looked at Papa Bear. "You slipped, Papa." Then she kissed Smurf on his cheek. "And you was on point. Sharp and aware, I had it all arranged to show the family how easily things could happen." Then she paused, took a deep breath, and added, "Bad news about it all, though, the Feds have ordered a hit on our entire family." She paused and waited for her words to sink in. "We all knew that slippers count. Papa, everything happens for a reason, but we've become a target. They wanna wipe the Walker family off the map and take out the Throne." She paused again. Watched her expectantly.

Majid wasn't expecting to hear anything like this at a formal dinner, but, being the man he was, and out of respect, he said, "We have nothing to worry about here in Dubai." He smiled, and then he said, "We're untouchable."

And he meant every word of it.

19

Over two hundred yards out in the gulf, a yacht was parked in the middle of the water with an anchor dropped just east of Amil's compound. Another smaller boat was behind it, occupied with four highly trained ex-Marines who were on call twenty-four hours a day for missions like this one. They worked strictly for the Government.

Tonight, it was dark; no moon and no stars. The four-man team was already dressed in swimsuits. There were carried encrypted Motorola phones. The yacht was only used as a decoy, just in case they were ambushed. Their opponent would think they were on the yacht instead of the smaller boat behind them. The federal Government was good. Hell, better than good. They were hot on the Walker family's trail, and they were dead serious. Each of the men was white, middle aged and well fit. Their height varied between six one and six five.

The lead man was lean with wide shoulders, his eyes were gray and alert. He slipped a pair of high-tech night vision goggles on his eyes. From his eyesight, everything turned a light illuminated green with traces of darker green and black. He could see four guards spread out near the rear entrance of the compound. Each of them dressed in black and their faces covered, all carrying mini assault rifles. The lead man took a small breath. He wanted to make this mission as simple as he possibly could. Everything would have to be clean, meaning everyone would have to die. All rules were out the door when things got this far.

The water were calm and peaceful, but the small boat still swayed a little. The guy to his left was stacked up with muscles like an action figure doll with a dull black elastic stretching over his whole body. In his hand, he held a remote device that resembled a joystick to an older ATARI game, except his had four small metal sticks. One was for driving the parked yacht. The next one controlled a fully automatic fifty caliber that was attached to the front end of the yacht, just enough for the barrel to fit through an opening. The trigger was at his fingertips.

At his touch, the yacht began moving west. They wanted to get as close to the shore at the rear of the estate as possible. There was a line of Palm trees around the wall of the compound. That would be their entrance once they got to land.

The lead man finally gave a signal. Immediately, they all put their mask, fins, and snorkel on. They took their hunting knives and brought their waterproof bags with silenced weapons and explosive devices.

The first three men hit the water quietly. They were about to hit the Walker and Khabir family at the same time.

BACK INSIDE AMIL'S ESTATE, everyone was sitting around the huge table. The Arabian women who served the food were pretty and well mannered. They served everything, including hot special dishes and exotic fruits. Smurf was relieved that Amil had tested him, but Fly took it personal, even though he hadn't said anything about it. He would, though, as soon as the opportunity presented itself.

Fly stood up from the table. Papa Bear looked at him, then he stood up and his eyes went to Smurf, who stood up as well. The three of them excused themselves from the table. Papa Bear led the way, and Smurf and Fly followed behind. They got to a huge high ceilinged corridor with floors made of rose-veined marble. They walked through another entrance that resembled a hotel lobby. Mirrors covered the walls, the floors were apricot marble and small dim lights decorated the ceilings. To the left was a three-piece sofa sectional, where the three of them found seats.

Papa Bear sat on the couch alone. Smurf sat down on the loveseat while Fly occupied the huge double stuffed chair. He leaned his cane against the side arm on his right. Then behind them, they heard footsteps against the marble floor.

Majid appeared and stopped at the threshold. In his thick eastern accent, he said, "An official meeting without me is like the United States going to war without the President's consent."

Papa Bear was facing him. He was already familiar with Majid, however, Fly and Smurf were not. Majid moved across the thick, carpeted floor once he entered. He sat down on the sofa next to Papa Bear and casually crossed his legs. His eyes darted around the room and looked each of them in their eyes. Majid knew their background, knew their history. He knew how Fly had lost his leg. He knew everything, because Amil had broken everything down to him and his wife. Besides, Amil could never do any wrong in their eyes.

"How's everybody doing?" Majid asked.

"Everything good. " Papa Bear said. "We were just about to formulate another business plan."

"Good. Whatever business you'll want to invest in, I'll back you financially."

Fly's antennas rose, then he cleared his throat, sat up to the edge of his seat and brought his cane in front of him. "We interested in fast money," he said.

Majid's eyes were on Fly, staring dead into his pupils. "Fast money comes quick, and goes quicker. What I got to offer is oil money." He fanned his hand. "I got friends in America in high places. We don't want to scar our faces with illegal activities."

Fly sat back in his chair again. He wanted in on the oil money also, but he needed work, and a lot of it. Then he said, "We need the Afghanistan connect with some keys of heroin. We not trying to do nothing here in Dubai, but we need the plug."

"Something like that..." Majid said. Then, he shook his head. "My people in the United States will talk bad about me. We got excellent connections, they'll never cross me."

Papa Bear smiled and looked at him. Then, from another part of the room, there was a light scream. That got everyone in the room's attention. Papa Bear got up and Majid followed. Smurf and Fly were in tow. They all hurried back toward the dining room where the women were, and to their surprise, there were ten Arabian guards in dark fatigues, boots and masks with weapons.

Majid said something in Arabic. The head guard tuned around and dropped the duffel bag that was slung across his shoulder in the middle of the floor and unzipped it. When he spread it open, Majid kneeled down on one knee and looked at the four decapitated heads inside.

The Arabian bodyguard looked at Majid, his eyes cold as steel from behind the mask he wore. Then he said in Arabic. "Americans."

Majid finished the sentence, "Just crossed us." He shook his head in pure disgust. Then he stood up and addressed the room, spreading his hands and masking his anger with a smile. "This calls for a celebration."

The room was filled with tension, but it was slowly dying

down. Majid was standing and looking around at everyone. When he got to Fly, he put his hand on his shoulder and looked him in his eyes. "If it's the connect you want, then it's the connect you'll get."

Fly kept his face expressionless and bowed his head in agreement. He knew it was time to adjust their hustle.

20

T wo hours had passed, and Majid was still somewhat upset. He thought about all the foreign affairs he'd had with the high end people back in the United States. In his head, he knew Americans and how they played. He'd given them oil supplies, funded operations under the table and across the table. Millions to charity, and he'd even had one of the biggest children's hospitals in the United States built. Now they'd sent their goons all the way to the United Arab Emirates to violate their code of honor. Majid was indeed a very smart man, and he was good at playing chess. The next move belonged to him.

After his people cleaned up the beach, and got rid of the boat, it was nearing midnight. The four dead American's bodies were removed from the compound and stored away in freezers across town. Majid, Falisa and Papa Bear were sitting alone in the rear of limousine on their way to another secluded area that Majid was sure of that the Feds couldn't find. Another reason Majid wanted to ride alone with Falisa and Papa Bear, is that he wanted to be clear on a few things with them.

Majid addressed them both at the same time. "I'll never be

a pawn on a chess board." His eyes darted from one to the other, and then he went on. "Where I'm about to take you two is an underground hideaway, but it's beautiful. Now, your son is interested in doing big things. Before I give the go ahead, I would like to hear it from you."

"Whatever my son asks for, give it to him." Falisa said, her voice easy but serious. She knew he was capable of handling business like that, and somewhere deep down inside, she felt like this was becoming more like a sport than enjoying the fruit of the hustle. Then she nodded her head, her eyes sparkled like diamonds underneath the interior lights. "He's reliable by far. And he got a good team behind him."

Silence hung in the air for a moment. Majid was a man of honor, and even more, a man of power. With his eyes still on Falisa, he slowly nodded. "And that's what I need to hear." Majid said to her. Then he cut his eyes over to Papa Bear, sat back against the comfortable leather seat and crossed his legs. "As of now, your life is in danger, and that's not good. I want the best for you and your family, Papa. But I think it's very much wise if the two of you would kind of stay out the way."

"Meaning?" Papa Bear asked.

"Disappear." Majid said boldly.

"I thought we were invisible over here," Papa Bear said. He rubbed his hands together.

Majid smiled while nodding his head at the same time. "Well, this time we will do it my way. The Feds are smart, but not that smart. Let's see if they'll come to the mountains." He paused, and then said, "Maybe we should give them something to do, since they have so much time on their hands."

The limousine was quiet except for the bulletproof tires that were rolling on the asphalt underneath them. Outside through the tinted windows, the illuminated skyline of Dubai was bringing a powerful impact on the entire scene, but the

limousine was moving fast. Just as fast as the armored
Hummer that was leading the convoy, and the three SUVs
behind them.

Majid cleared his throat. His eyes were on Papa Bear, then
he cut them toward Falisa and back to Papa again. "You two
seem very much alike, in a good way. My question is, why aren't
you married?"

Falisa smiled, her shoulders shrugged a little while slowly
turning her head to face Papa Bear. "Good question. Why aren't
we married?"

"The timing just hasn't been right." Papa Bear said calmly.
He grabbed Falisa's hand and brought it up to his face, kissed
the back of it and looked at her and then to Majid.

Majid picked up the phone inside the console, punched a
single digit number. A voice answered from the other end in
Arabic. Majid said a few words in a language that Papa nor
Falisa spoke. When he hung up, there was a smile on his face.
Then all he said was, "Allah has blessed you both."

THE FOLLOWING AFTERNOON, Fly, Smurf, Amil and Iris were all
gathered inside a private location. The building was made out
of gray cinder blocks and sitting on two hundred acres of
private land owned by relatives of Majid. Inside this particular
room that was a shaped like an octagon, they sat around a
marble table in high backed comfortable leather swivels. While
they waited for their new connect to arrive, Amil broke the
silence while scrolling through her computer. "Washington D.C
is a major heroin city," she said while scanning the computer
screen.

She tapped the keys again and read off what popped up
next. "Baltimore, Maryland, New York City, New Orleans, San
Francisco..." She paused. Her lips pressed tight together, and

then her eyes went from one side of the computer screen to the other.

She read for another three minutes while the rest of the room sat quietly. Elbows on the table, fingertips pressed together, eyes on Amil.

Finally, she looked up from the screen and smiled at them. "The numbers should be good if we can get a decent price on the keys. The going rate for a kilo of heroin from Afghanistan is roughly two thousand dollars. We need to get them cheaper, because it's gonna cost to play."

"Let's lay out a rough estimate figure." Fly said, looking at Amil.

Amil's eyes were back on the computer screen, and before she could respond, a knock came from the door behind her. She got up immediately, went to the door, and opened it. A short Middle Eastern man in his early fifties with intelligent brown eyes that were sunken deep into their sockets stood in the doorway. His jaws were strong and he had a thick neck. Dressed in American clothes, denim jeans, a crisp button up shirt, he carried a leather briefcase in his left hand.

He gave his right hand to Amil. She took it, and he said in low soft tone of voice, "Evening ma'am. I'm Pakistan."

Amil smiled, bowed her head, stepped to the side, and allowed him to come in. Amil closed the door behind him. Pakistan stood there and waited for her before he moved.

She went past him and walked back toward the table. "This is Pakistan, everyone."

Pakistan went around the table, shaking everyone's hand. They exchanged names and he finally took one of the available sets, set the briefcase on top of the table, snapped the locks, and lifted the lid. Inside, there was one kilo of heroin wrapped in tight transparent plastic. He pulled it out and held it up in his hand. Then he handed the white compressed square brick to Amil.

She turned it over from one side to the other, staring and examining it. "What's our price?" she asked.

Pakistan looked around the table at everyone. "Normally, fifteen hundred a kilo. Majid say your price is seven hundred. However, you'll have to pay an additional one thousand a key to get through Iran and to Turkey. But in the United States and Europe, you'll get fifty thousand a piece and that's wholesale."

Smurf was watching Pakistan and doing the numbers in his head at the same time. The numbers sounded so good that it was unbelievable. He looked at Fly. Iris was next to him with a laptop computer in front of her. She was looking at the screen, but Fly and Smurf were staring at each other.

Smurf turned his mouth up and pressed his lips together as if he was impressed, and then he said, "So basically, we move one thousand bricks of heroin, we pull in five hundred million?"

Pakistan looked over at him, his deep sunken eyes fixed directly on Smurf. "Correct." was all he said.

"Well, we want two tons. Two separate shipments. That should be about forty four hundred kilos. I already have the available stash spot for that amount. However, I'm interested in cocaine too if you can get it for me. These other people just won't budge." Amil said.

Pakistan looked to Amil. "We can get you whatever you want, Amil. And we can get it to wherever you need it to go. You sure you got a good hiding spot?"

Amil smiled. "Trust me on this." Then she asked one last question. "Do you think I can get my own stamp on the kilos?"

"Sure, no problem." Pakistan said. He rubbed the front face of the kilo of heroin. "Your stamp will go right here. What do you want it to be?"

Without hesitation, Amil said, "My face."

Everyone around the table looked at her as if she was crazy. And she was.

21

N early a month later, Agent Edgar was sitting behind his desk at his home in Denver Colorado. On the wall, he had black and white photos of Amil and Fly. There were also photos of Falisa, Papa Bear, and Smurf. There wasn't any of Iris, because he didn't know what she looked like. On his desk in front of him were the same files of information, only these were copies. Paul Edgar was a smart man, but in his years of being a federal agent, he hadn't seen anything like this before.

With a long, drawn out deep breath, he pushed himself back from his desk and stood up. He wore a white tee shirt underneath a powder blue button up shirt that was opened and untucked. He rubbed his hand over his face and looked back over the photos once again. He couldn't let it go, he wanted this case, hell he still wants it now. Then he tried to shake it away.

Paul Edgar walked out of his office and into the hallway. His home was a four bedroom with a huge dining room, a great room, and a big kitchen. Two car garage, three bathrooms and private fenced in yard that was about four acres with in ground swimming pool. Paul made a right down the hallway and walked into the small sitting area. There was a sofa to his left, and a glass top coffee table. He moved through it and went into the kitchen. His wife was standing at the sink drying a few dishes with a cloth. He tip toed up behind her and wrapped his hands round her waist. She jumped, then she relaxed to his touch.

Paul moved her hair away from her neck and softly kissed her there. She closed her eyes and rested her head against his shoulder. "I'm taking you out to lunch. Me and you, no interruptions."

His wife turned around and faced him, her face was pink and clean. She smiled. "Are you sure you got time, Paul?" She needed clarity because he was always flying in and out at the spur of the moment.

Paul had his mind made up. He was seeing his marriage bond becoming weaker, so today, he would set everything aside for his wife and spend some time with her. Paul leaned in and kissed her lips, her eyes closed and he slipped his tongue inside her mouth. "Get dressed," he mumbled.

She pulled away from him and blushed even harder, nearly embarrassed that her nipples were hard and pressing through her cotton shirt. She wrapped her arms around herself and moved around him, backing away with a blushing smile.

"I'm going to get ready." She said, and then faded away from his eyesight.

Paul walked outside through the glass patio doors. The Denver, Colorado air was thin. It wasn't cold, nor was it hot. Paul enjoyed the view from the rear of his home. Across his property and in the distance, he could see the mountains covered by a thin layer of fog. Paul took a deep breath and stood out there for nearly fifteen minutes, lost in thought. He was thinking about his career as a DEA agent, how he was played for a fool by the Walker family. That alone made his credibility level drop a couple notches with the director of his division.

He pushed the thought as far away from his mind as possible. Then he turned around and walked inside. When he got to his bedroom, his wife was coming out the bathroom. Her hair was damp and brushed toward the back, with a thick white terry cloth robe wrapped around her body. She looked gorgeous.

Paul couldn't keep his eyes away from his wife. Her name was Sarah, but he just addressed her as plain old Honey. Before he headed into the bathroom to shower and dress, he grabbed her hand, pulled her close to him and held her close, rubbing his nose against hers. She couldn't help but to blush. He kissed her, backed way and walked into the bathroom.

Sarah went to her dresser, removed her robe and looked at her body in the mirror. Her nipples were rose-pink and the size of erasers. She had a gently curved body that was desperately in need of a tan. She slipped on a pair of lace panties, walked to the walk-in closet, and removed a cream dress from a suit bag.

Ten minutes later, she was dressed.

Paul was out of the shower and slowly getting dressed himself. He was casual, dress pants and hard bottom shoes, a white button up shirt and a nice tie. He looked at himself in the mirror while tying his tie.

He turned to face Sarah. "Where you wanna eat at?"

She was putting on her earrings. "Anywhere I want?" She asked him with a smile.

"Your choice, honey." Paul said again. "Me personally, I got a taste for lobster tail and steak."

"And a little wine..."

"Definitely wine." he said. "Now let's get going before the kids get out of school."

Sarah went to the mirror and touched up her face with makeup and lipstick.

Outside in their three-car garage, Sarah got on the passenger side of their Tahoe while Paul got on the driver side. He closed his door, looked over at his wife. "No disturbance," he said and started the engine. The remote for the garage door was clamped to his sun visor. He touched the button and the bay door behind him began to roll up. The bright daylight spilled into the garage. He pulled the gear selector into reverse and began easing out backwards.

"I'm so excited." Sarah said, looking at herself in the mirror, pressing her lips together to assure her that her rose red lipstick was evenly across her lips. She closed her small hand held kit and looked at Paul when his cell phone lit up and buzzed at the same time.

Sarah's eyes were on the phone. It rang once... twice... a third time.

Her eyes cut up at him after the fourth ring, and that's when he answered it. Just as he put the phone up to his face, he read the unpleasant facial expression from his wife. It didn't matter who was on the other end of his phone, because he wasn't about to change his plans.

"Yes, Agent Edgar speaking." He put his foot on the brake and stopped the SUV at the end of the driveway.

"Agent Edgar, how's it going? This is Amil Walker again, and I'm really sorry to bother you."

"How did you get this number?" he asked her coldly. He was turning beet red from the neck up.

"Listen to me sir, I'm about to change your life and probably get you a couple rewards or something. But you got to get there."

"Get where? What is it?"

"Five hundred kilos of heroin is waiting for you at LAX airport right now. No tricks. No games. Now do you want the bust or what?"

Paul began sweating around his neck and quickly rubbed

his hand underneath his shirt collar. He looked at Sarah, who was now looking out the window at her front lawn. He knew how she was feeling, and she was probably cursing him out. He needed this bust, and figured she'd understand.

"Where do I need to go?"

All Sarah could do was shake her head in disgust.

22

Two hours later, Paul Edgar was landing at LAX. When he got off the plane, three federal agents were waiting for him at the gate, two males and one female. The two men were dressed casually, dark suits, white shirts, blue ties and tinted shades. The female federal agent was in a dark blue skirt that came past her knees. She wore a matching jacket over a white blouse. After Paul introduced himself to them, they all followed his lead and walked through the airport. Paul went to the luggage carrousel and stood there, staring at the sea of people. He slipped on his shades, put his hands on his waist, and in the next thirty seconds, his phone rang. He removed it from the clamp on his belt and answered it. "Edgar speaking."

"There's a black Hummer limousine parked in front of the airport. Go to it. There's two Samsonite suitcases in the back, just for you. You can thank me later." Amil said and then the line went dead.

Paul Edgar didn't waste any time at all. Soon as the call disconnected, he began walking toward the exit doors. The other three agents were right with him. Once they got outside, he looked to his left, and just as promised, there was a long black Hummer double parked. It was clean, shiny black with tinted windows. Paul pulled his gun and carefully walked up to the driver side window and looked in.

The other agents looked in also. They were being careful at the same time. Paul Edgar had called in to the DEA office in LA to assist him, since it was their jurisdiction.

Paul walked to the rear door and looked at the handle before opening it. He was still somewhat undecided for several reasons. One was Amil Walker. Two was Amil Walker, and three was Amil Walker. When he finally shook the negative thoughts away, he opened the driver side rear door. A strong odor hit his nose immediately, but there on the floor was two huge suitcases. Paul climbed inside and one of the other agents opened the opposite side rear door.

Paul unzipped the first suitcase, flipped the top up, and to his surprise, there were neat stacks of kilos of heroin. Paul removed one of them and looked at the top front face of it. There was a design that appeared to be the image of something like a blueprint. But instead, it was in the color pink and formed in the shape of a circle with a white background. He tore the paper off, put it to this nose to assure that it was official, and sighed.

When he looked up at the other agent across from him, a smile spread across his face. "Call the media. We going live with this one."

TWO HOURS LATER, Paul Edgar had LAX in an uproar. Federal agents were everywhere around the airport. News reporters and cameramen were spilling in from every direction. Paul was talking with a news reporter from LA Times and another one from CNN. Five hundred kilos of heroin were stacked up behind him, all white with the pink print design stamped in the middle. A bust like this would put him in a better position. His superiors had questioned him about the anonymous caller, and to his own surprise, he didn't tell them that it was Amil. Hell, he didn't even know who it was. For all he knew, it could've been any female voice. He would worry about that later. As of now, the cameras were rolling and flashing, and his next stop would be Quantico and then Washington DC.

Paul Edgar took his last picture, posing with the five hundred kilos of heroin. He stood on one side and the Chief of Police in LA was standing on the opposite side with a wide smile on his face. Why wouldn't he? A bust like this was something everybody wanted a piece of.

"Say cheese." The man behind the camera said. Then he snapped the picture.

Paul Edgar had been sucked up into Amil's world, and he didn't even know it.

23

B altimore Maryland was a rough city with a high crime rate, from the west side to the east side. With areas like Edmondson Village, Cherry Hill, and Harlem Park to name a few. But the main thing was that Baltimore was the heroin capitol of the United States. On this particular day, the skies were gray and gloomy looking, and the streets were wet. On the Westside of Baltimore, inside a small two bedroom apartment, was a young street hustler and goon who went by the name, Cam. His first name was Cory, but most of the people from the streets called him Cam.

Cam lived in an apartment with his sister, who had two kids that were ages three and four, boy and a girl. Cam was nineteen years old and a stone cold killer that took hits for a price of anywhere between five hundred and five thousand dollars. It all depended on who was ordering the hit. Inside his bedroom, he sat at the foot of his full sized bed with a Nike shoebox in his lap, thumbing through his life savings, which was seventeen hundred dollars in cash, three bundles of heroin, and a small .380 handgun that was for his personal use only.

Cam sat the box on the bed next to him, stood up, stretched, and yawned. He was a bony teenager, stood five eleven, and weighed no more than one hundred and forty pounds. He had huge hands and a long face with sleepy looking eyes. He wore a short, two inch afro that was nappy and unkempt, and he dressed in baggy jeans, a white fitted tank tops, and a few pieces of jewelry that were on back of the closet door. He was growing a beard, but it wasn't full, and mostly in patches.

He smiled at himself, thinking about the earlier phone call he had received from a guy across town who was plugged in with a crew of drug traffickers from New York. The guy across town was ruthless and young, just like Cam. Except he was two years older than Cam, and moved nearly a quarter key of heroin between Baltimore and DC a week. That meant he was seeing a couple of dollars. With the street money coming in, his associate took on the alias, Sosa, mimicking the Colombian from the movie, *Scarface*.

Cam was ready for whatever, because at his age, coming up in a poverty-stricken environment like Baltimore, nothing too much mattered but coming up. He took his clothes off and took a quick shower. Ten minutes later, he was out with a towel wrapped around his waist. Cam slipped into a pair of boxer briefs, a clean pair of jeans, another white tank top and a baby blue Polo button up shirt. From his closet, he removed a pair of all white low cut Air Force Ones. After he was completely dressed, he removed a short stock AK-47 from under his bed, stuffed it in a nylon duffel bag and slung it over his shoulder.

He walked to the mirror and looked at himself once again. Satisfied.

When he got outside, cars passed by, the tires hissing against the slick-wet asphalt. Then a black Jaguar with tinted windows and factory rims pulled up and stopped next to the curb beside him. Cam looked at the car and saw his people, Sosa, in the passenger side behind the tint. Cam got in the backseat, sank into the comfortable leather, and closed the door. The inside of the Jaguar smelled like strong exotic mari-juana mixed with a strawberry air freshener. The guy behind the wheel pulled off into traffic.

Sosa turned around and reached his hand out toward Cam. "Wuss up, main man?"

Cam dapped him up, then took the bag and set it on the seat next to him. "I'm easy. What up. What we got?"

Sosa was still looking at him, then he pulled out a Newport and fired it up. He turned around and faced the front, while the driver drove on in silence. While the young cat, Sosa, watched he streets, he said, "Got a couple of new people in town that want in on some B-more money." He blew out a stream of smoke.

"So what's the business?"

"We bout to go downtown and meet them. See what they talking bout. If they ain't talkin' bout no numbers, they ain't talkin' bout nothing."

He paused and then went on. "I called on you because you like my best shooter I got. Just can't trust anybody today to watch ya' back. You feel me, main man?"

"Yeah, I'm witcha. I'm with whatever, I'm trying to eat." Cam said and unzipped his duffel bag then calmly removed the short AK-47 and laid it across his lap just as the car was coming to a halt at a four way red light.

Sosa noticed his movement from the rearview, but he was safe with Cam, because he knew he could trust him. They stared out the window, watching the small circle of goons that hung out on the corner in front of a small pizza parlor. When the light turned green, the driver took off again. Sosa cracked his window two inches and allowed the smoke to seep out of the car. They rode in silence for another ten minutes, then Sosa's cell phone rang. He brought it up to his face.

"Hello." he said in his soft voice.

"Hello, friend." An unknown voice said from the other end.

"What I would like for you to do is come to the National Aquarium. From there, you'll be approached by my assistant, and he'll guide you to the water taxi. Once you're on the water taxi, I'll call you back. Thanks for your time, Mr. Sosa." Then the line went dead.

Sosa was so caught up in the conversation that his cigarette had gone out without him noticing. He thumped the butt out the window and set his phone in his lap. He looked to his driver, who was focused on the road, his head and eyes straight forward and his fingers were laced around the steering column. "Main man, go to the big Aquarium." was all he said.

His main man, as he referred to him, gave one quick nod of the head and straightened himself up as if he was going to meet the mayor or something.

Sosa turned his small frame half way around in his seat and looked back at Cam. "You ever been on a water taxi before?"

"I don't even know what da' fuck dat is, main man." Cam said and laughed. He really didn't, that was something of no interest to him. Therefore, he couldn't care less.

The driver spoke for the first time. "Water taxis are cool. Traveling from spot to spot, just on a boat. They be having yachts out there too. Boss shit for a nigga and his bitch."

"Okay," Sosa said and turned back toward the front.

He looked through the front windshield, as he thought to himself, *we are really about to get on for real.* The rest of the way to their destination, the entire car was silent.

24

Night was creeping fast as they arrived at the National Aquarium in Baltimore. The driver parked in an empty space between a Volvo and a minivan. Cam was the first one to step out with the duffel bag containing the AK slung over his shoulder. The National Aquarium was a huge building with glass everywhere, and it threw off a soft light across the parking lot.

Sosa stepped out and looked around, scanning the area, including where the boats and water were. The pier was just ahead, in walking distance. Then out of nowhere, Pakistan appeared, simply dressed in denim jeans, a denim jacket, and steel toe boots. He appeared to be the assistant.

"Good evening," he said, while walking around the rear of the car to where Cam and Sosa stood. "First of all, no weapons beyond this point." He paused, and his eyes went straight to Sosa. "Only the two of you, correct?" His Arabian accent was thick.

Sosa nodded, then he reached under his shirt and pulled out a seventeen round .9MM and tossed it on the front seat. Cam followed and put the bag on the floor in the back.

When the door closed, Pakistan started walking. "Come with me, gentlemen," he said and headed in the direction of the pier.

They boarded a water taxi, which took them to another pier. The three of them exited the boat. Ten minutes later, they were walking through the lobby of the Baltimore Marriott Waterfront. This particular hotel is located next to the Baltimore harbor. From the lobby, they took one of the elevators to the thirtieth floor, and Pakistan put his key into the room door. Sosa and Cam were standing behind him; nobody said a word.

When Pakistan opened the door, they all filed inside and closed it behind them. The room was a sight for sore eyes, giving off a casual atmosphere with just the right amount of elegance. Pakistan showed them inside. "Gentlemen, if you would make yourself at home," he said, and then he went back toward the front door. He turned and faced them before he left. "You'll receive a call in less than an hour." He stood there and waited to see if either of them had anything to say. When no one said anything, he went through the door and closed it behind him.

Cam looked at Sosa, a surprised expression plastered over his face. He said in a low whispered tone, "Man, this might be the plug fa'real."

Sosa didn't respond; he was a little cocky at times. He turned his head toward Cam, stared in his eyes for a couple of seconds, and then he said, "Yeah, let'em fuck around and be soft and put anything over ten bricks in my hand, and they can kiss my baby good bye." He stood from the couch where he'd just sat down and walked over toward a bar on the left wall.

Cam was still standing. He hoped he didn't hear what he thought he just heard. Kiss the baby meant that he was going to vanish on the connect. Cam walked over to the bar and stood opposite of Sosa. "Main man, this the opportunity of a life time, and I—"

"Let me fuck this chicken, brah." Sosa said, cutting Cam off mid-sentence.

He pulled a small bottle of Patron from the bar, unscrewed the top, and poured it down his throat. He looked back at Cam.

Cam held his tongue and took a tour through the room. They were inside one of the executive king suites. Cam went to the huge window and pulled the string. The drapes parted, revealing a spectacular the view of the city of Baltimore.

Cam looked back at Sosa. "Damn," he said, and then he pointed at the illuminated skyline. "Look at this shit."

"I'm not interested." Sosa said, then he added, "We don't even know these people, nigga, and you getting comfortable already."

The hotel room phone rang and ended Cam and Sosa's conversation. Cam looked around the room and noticed the phone sitting on an end table next to the loveseat. He walked over to it and removed it from the charger. "Hello.'

"Downstairs at the Kozmo's Lounge. You'll be there in thirty minutes, okay."

The line went dead. At least it was a woman's voice this time. That made Sosa angry. He hated to feel like a peon, but in this case, he'd accept it until further notice. He definitely had a plan, and it would surely get him on top.

When he hung the phone up, he looked at Cam. It was no surprise that he was already watching him. "That was the call."

No more than fifteen minutes later, a handsome and well-groomed Spanish man in a two-piece suit, dress shirt, and dark tie was escorting Sosa and Cam through Kozmo's lounge. When they got to the table for four, Amil was there waiting in one of the comfortable chairs. Next to her was Pakistan. They stood nearly at the same time. Amil was dressed in traditional

Muslim garb, making it even harder for her to be recognized. Her head was covered with a hijab and her body was concealed behind a black over garment. She shook hands with the young guy, Sosa, first.

Amil gave him a smile. "Hello." she said.

Sosa nodded and fixed a fake grin on his face.

"Have a seat," Amil said politely.

She released his hand and turned her attention toward Cam. Amil extended her hand to him and gave him a smile.

Cam grabbed her hand and smiled at her while he shook it. When the four of them sat down around the circular tables, a waiter appeared. He didn't take long, mainly because Amil ordered water for everyone.

When the waiter left, Amil got straight to business. Her eyes went to Sosa and she said, "You have very impressive track record around here in the city of Baltimore."

"How did you hear about me?" he asked. His tone was cocky.

"I keep my ear to the streets. However, I'm interested in you because I know you can move heroin locally. But what I'm looking for is someone that can handle the entire east coast.

Sosa smiled again, this time it was genuine. His eyes were sparkling and he didn't know it. He sat up, clearly more interested now. "The whole east coast?"

"One hundred keys. Can you handle that? This opportunity will make you a very rich man. Are you interested?"

"I'm interested, I can handle it," he said anxiously.

"Good."

She turned her attention to Cam. Her eyes looked into his. She put her elbows on the table and locked her fingers between each other. "And who do we have here?"

"I'm Cam," he said.

"He my main man. He gonna be working with me." Sosa interrupted.

"Cool." Amil said, as cheerful as can be. She felt that these two could handle that business. "We gonna eat, we gonna get the both of you in position where you need to be."

Sosa and Cam both allowed their faces to brighten. News like this was something any street hustler could only dream about. Just then, the waiter reappeared with the tray of four glasses of ice water. He sat one glass in front of each of them. "Anything else, Ma'am?" He looked straight at Amil and asked.

Amil flashed the waiter a beautiful smile and picked up her glass. "This will be it. Thank you so much."

The waiter bowed his head at her, turned on his heels, and walked off. Amil's eyes followed him until he was out of her sight, then she looked back at Sosa, sipped her water, swallowed and sat her glass back down on the table. "So, Sosa, how do you plan on selling one hundred kilos of heroin?" she asked. "But before you answer that question," she looked at Pakistan. "Give me a few minutes. Take Cam with you, and me and Sosa will be up in a moment."

Pakistan had the calmest look on his face when he pushed the chair out and stood up. Cam stood up too. Together, they threaded through the sea of tables and people.

25

Pakistan stepped off the elevator first, then Cam came out behind him. Together, they walked side by side to the room they'd just left. Pakistan entered his card key, the small green light came on and he opened the door and stepped inside. Cam was right behind him on his heels. When Pakistan locked the door, Cam noticed two more men sitting in the living room on the sofas that were now covered with thick plastic.

Cam looked down to the floor and noticed that the entire carpet was covered with thick plastic, and duct taped carefully around the edges. The walls were all covered with plastic, the drapes were closed, and beyond that, the two gentlemen that were sitting down, were watching him like a Hawk.

Pakistan placed his hand on Cam's back when he noticed the worried look in his eyes. "Have a seat." He almost pushed him, just enough to let him know he needed to take a seat.

Cam moved over to the available chair, in the circle of the other two gentlemen who were dressed in tuxedos, all black and black bow ties. They didn't look American to Cam, even though they were white. They were Amil's business associates, and they were nothing more than professional killers.

Cam cleared his throat, his eyes darting between both of them. He looked at Pakistan, who was sitting next to one the killers, and asked, "What's up, brah?" He looked around at everything covered in plastic. "What's this about?"

"Your friend, Sosa." Pakistan said calmly. "We got your conversation from earlier recorded." He shrugged, then he took a cigar from the gentleman next to him. Not another word was said until he fired the cigar up.

Cam got instantly nervous, his eyebrows bunched together. The wheels started spinning immediately. The cigar smoke was now circulating in the room.

Pakistan stood up and walked around the chair to where Cam sat. Cam looked back at him, fear was in his eyes, but Pakistan placed his hands on each of his shoulders while he held the cigar clenched between his teeth. "Relax, you're the loyal one, and you're the one we gonna keep." He began massaging his shoulders and relaxing Cam.

The other two gentlemen still hadn't said one word, they really didn't have that deadly killer look, maybe because they were calm about the situation. Most killers were always calm anyway.

Pakistan moved back around, his cigar between his thumb and index finger. He stood in the middle of the floor, the plastic rattling underneath his feet. He looked at Cam and said, "I can change your life in the blink of an eye. You'll be the wealthiest street entrepreneur on the east. But first, you have to get rid of your friend, Sosa. He's dead weight to us."

He then took a few steps backwards and found his seat again, his eyes fixed on Cam. He pulled on the cigar again, and allowed the smoke to stream around his face. Pakistan was as deadly and treacherous as they came, and Cam was feeling that in this hotel room.

He finally took a deep breath and relaxed. "I'm ready," he said.

"Good decision." Pakistan said and stood up again. He smelled like cigar smoke, then he disappeared into the bedroom. When he came back, he was holding a Colombian necktie, which was a mixture of silk and fishing line woven together with a loop on each end for the hands to go through. When he got back to Cam, he dropped it in his lap, then he sat back down in his same seat.

The other two gentlemen still hadn't said one word, only looking, nothing more. This would be a test for Cam, because he had never killed anybody with anything except a gun. When he picked up the Colombian necktie, he eased his hands in the loops on each end, examining it. Pakistan could tell he didn't know how to use it, so he stood again, moved over to Cam, and told him to stand up.

He did, still holding the murder weapon. Pakistan then sat down in the chair where Cam had been sitting. He looked up at Cam. "Now, slip it around my neck," he said, and turned around in the chair.

Cam moved behind him in the chair and eased the necktie carefully around his neck. His eyes went to the two gentlemen. He wasn't comfortable with doing this in front of them, but this was it, and there was no turning back.

"Okay." Pakistan said. "Now cross your hands."

Cam carefully crossed his hands, not putting any pressure on his neck. Then he realized how it would go and was satisfied immediately. He removed the necktie.

Pakistan stood up and walked to the phone. He picked it up and pressed the on button. Someone answered on the other end and Pakistan said, "Green light."

He hung the phone up.

~

DOWNSTAIRS, Amil and Sosa were having a good conversation when the waiter appeared. Amil's eyes cut up at him. He flashed her a smile with an even set of white teeth. "Ma'am, your call has come." He said, then his head bowed. "Can I get either of you anything else to before you leave?"

Amil looked at Sosa. "You want anything else?"

Sosa squinted; he wanted to tell her what he really wanted. All of the above. Then he responded, "If you good, I'm good." he said, trying to sound sexy. Even allowing a small sexy grin.

Amil caught it. She stood up, still smiling at him while he stood too. "Business first," she said and winked at him. On the table was a basket of delicious bread sticks with cheese filling on the inside. Sosa picked up two of them and fell in stride next to Amil.

When they got upstairs to the room, Pakistan was waiting at the door for them. Amil walked inside first. When Pakistan stepped back, Sosa came in, so caught up in himself and Amil, that he didn't even notice the entire room was covered in plastic. When he got further inside, he noticed Cam and the two well-dressed gentlemen were holding conversation. Then everything got quiet.

Pakistan closed the door. It caught the latch and locked. When he turned around and faced the room, Amil went to the left and found a seat in a leather chair that was covered in plastic also. Pakistan showed Sosa to the available chair where they'd just got finished demonstrating how they would kill him.

When he sat down, there were two separate kilos of heroin sitting on the table in the center of them all. His eyes immediately flew to them. That told him that these people were dead serious about their business. Even Amil told him downstairs that he would definitely be in position in a short time.

Then out of nowhere, a recorded voice came from a small hand-held device that Pakistan produced. He sat it on top of one of the kilos:

Man, this might be the plug fa'real.

Yeah, let'em fuck around and be soft and put anything over ten bricks in my hands, and they can kiss the baby goodbye.

Silence.

Main man, this the opportunity of a life time and I—

Let me fuck this chicken, brah.

Pakistan pressed the stop button and the entire hotel room was silent.

Amil cleared her throat and said, "The number one leading cause of death in young African Americans is running their mouth too much." Her eyes were fixed directly on Sosa.

Just then, Cam stood up. "Bathroom." was all he said.

When he went around the chair where Sosa was sitting, he slipped the necktie around his neck so quick he didn't know what to do. Sosa began kicking and struggling immediately. The other two gentlemen got up, each one of them forcefully holding his arms down. He kicked the table over and Amil just sat there and watched while Cam slowly choked him to his death.

And just that quickly, Cam was now a Made Man.

26

Time was moving, and so was the product that Amil had. Nearly three months went by and Amil and Pakistan traveled to every major drug capitol in the United States, looking for prospects like Cam. They had Chicago, New York, Miami, Atlanta, and a couple of cities on the West Coast. There was an official street team that she'd put together in New Mexico. Amil was a risk taker, mainly because she wanted to be hands on with her entrepreneural street skills, except hers were all the way on another level.

Through the Majid family alone, Amil had purchased a fleet of private jets. Ten of them to be exact, some fancy G-5's, which were all built with a million dollar stash inside the walls and the engines of the jets. Each private jet was equipped to hold two hundred kilos with no problem.

Amil, also had two huge oil tankers that traveled and moved heroin and cocaine through the water, but she had that just for her brother, Fly, and Iris where they distributed kilos of both to the Jamaicans in London and their street connect in Paris. Smurf moved with them, and they were collecting millions on a weekly basis and moving all the money straight to Dubai where Falisa and Papa Bear lived like a royal family in a hidden area.

This was just a portion of Amil's so called pink print. Today, it was six minutes after five in the morning, and she was in Colorado. Not far from downtown, there was huge warehouse building that had been up for sale for the past year. It was definitely in a nice area of Denver, sitting in the center of several restaurants, hotels and other businesses. Amil and her new guardian, Pakistan, were sitting around a small square table with fold out legs. Their chairs were metal fold out. The ground was covered with raw concrete and the room gave off a stale mildew odor that would normally make Amil's nose crinkle, but she was used to nearly all types of smells now.

On the small table, Pakistan had a cool million dollars in cash tucked inside an aluminum briefcase. In the corner, to the right of him was a four-foot tall wooden peanut shaped Styrofoam ball. To the left was a suitcase, the biggest one that came with a set. It held close to forty kilos of cocaine. Each one individually wrapped and stacked. Amil looked at her watch. Another five minutes had passed quickly.

Just then, Pakistan's phone rang, only vibrating inside the deep left pocket of his jeans. He removed it and answered it. Two simple words came from the other end. "All clear."

Pakistan ended the call and looked over at Amil, who was patiently waiting. Pakistan nodded.

Amil pushed her chair backwards and stood up. She removed a specially made cloth from her pocket that wiped away any and all fingerprints. She went around the warehouse wiping everything from the table, to the chairs, the suitcase and the door handles.

Pakistan stood up; this guy was always calm and cool with anything he did. He looked at Amil, she was careful and just as calm as he was. After she'd completed her process, both of them took a side metal door that led them to a separate garage that was spacious and smelled of wet, damp concrete. There was a brand new Mercedes Benz four-door sedan with Colorado license plates. In the front seat of the car was two males, both with a bullet to the back of their heads. The guy in the driver seat was leaning forward, his head pressed against the steering column. The unknown guy in the passenger seat was slumped also, except he was leaning sideways with his head pressed against the window, as if he was peacefully sleeping. A spray of blood streaked the glass.

Amil walked around like she'd forgotten something. Her eyes went to Pakistan. He was much older and fiercer, but judging him from his appearance, he looked soft and harmless. That's one of the reasons Amil chose him as her assistant. However, today, Amil had a new position for Pakistan to play. Pakistan's eyes were on her, glistening with excitement, then he smiled, assuring her that he was ready. She pulled out an untraceable phone and handed it to him.

Amil checked her watch. They still had a few hours delay, so they waited.

LATER THAT SAME EVENING, Paul Edgar and his wife, Sarah, were dressed formally. He was in a tuxedo and she was in a strapless dress and heels, sitting across from each other at a restaurant called Fogo de Chao. Their table was square and draped with a white cloth. The atmosphere was elegant and relaxing, candles were lit on the table and their choice of meal for this evening was Corduroy Lamb imported straight from New Zealand, with tender lamb chops, jumbo Asparagus, shitake mushroom, twenty-four-month aged parmesan and artisan bread. The aroma was unexplainable, and they actually had vintage red wine to accompany their meal.

Paul bit into a piece of the tender meat and it nearly melted in his mouth. He looked across at Sarah while chewing, and said, "I swear, I love this place." He chewed a couple of times and swallowed.

She smiled, thankful that they could finally have a peaceful dinner together without any unnecessary disturbance. Then in a polite manner, she picked up one of the jumbo asparagus and bit down into it. She gave her husband the most seductive look that she could. "And I love you, Paul. But honey, you're over working yourself. I really think you deserve a vacation." Her voice was soft and sincere.

Paul slowly nodded in agreement, picked up his glass of wine and sipped from it. "Big considerations," he said, his eyes on hers, watching her as she eased her elbows up on the table. Her wedding band sparkled underneath the soft lighting and flickering candles.

Paul reached across the table with his free hand and grabbed her hand. She smiled. He brought it up to his mouth and kissed the diamond ring, then kissed the back of her fingers. They were long and delicate.

Both of them were lost in thought and staring into each other's eyes. Around the restaurant, there were other couples sitting at their tables. Waiters were weaving through the room; light chatter filled the elegant atmosphere. Then out of nowhere, a young beautiful blond stood up and began screaming at the man that was sitting across from her.

Immediately, Paul turned his head in the direction of the commotion. He couldn't help but to notice how beautiful the young lady was. Her body was sculpted as if she'd been molded by hand. She was in an expensive white dress and high heels, and yelling at the white guy in front of her in another language.

He sat quiet and calmly, stirring around a couple of ice cubes in a glass half filled with alcohol. Then Paul heard her say loud and clear. "You're a coward murderer." She spat in his face.

Several Fogo de Chao employees began to gather around their table. Paul stood up. Sarah felt disgusted that he had to go intervene in other people's affairs while they were out on a date. She sat back in her chair, folded her arms across her chest, and slowly shook her head.

This is it, she said to herself. *You'd better not, Paul.* Her eyes squinted as she watched him walk away, reaching for his wallet badge.

27

Paul Edgar had his badge in his hand as he made his way through the crowd. Everyone in the restaurant was looking in the direction of the blond who was still standing over the man, angrily calling him a coward murderer. When Paul got to her, he flashed his federal wallet badge at her. She got quiet instantly. Her eyes were moist as she moved behind Paul and grabbed his arm while pointing in the direction of the white guy in the all-white linen suit. He had a surprised look on his face, as if he didn't know what she was talking about. He had gray eyes and black oily hair and was clean shaven.

"What's going on here?" Paul asked.

The guy looked at Paul and said, "Listen, let me explain—"

"No, let me explain," The girl said from behind him. "He's a coward murderer, and I can take you to the bodies and everything else."

Paul looked at her, stared blankly for a couple seconds then he looked at the guy who was looking just as confused.

"Sir, I haven't the slightest idea what she's talking about. I'm not sure if you know me or not, but my father is the head prose-

cutor in this town. I don't have anything to do with what she's
talking about."

Restaurant patrons were standing around, looking in pure
shock at what the girl was telling them. The girl was crying
now, her eyeliner streaking down her face. "Officer, it's a warehouse over on Colfax Avenue, where everything is at. Two men
dead for no reason. Guns and drugs."

That was enough to make Paul Edgar remove his gun from
his holster. Then he pulled out his phone and made a call.

WITHIN THE NEXT TWO HOURS, there were ATF, DEA, and local
Denver police crowded inside the warehouse on Colfax. Paul
Edgar was the lead on this case. He was still dressed in his
tuxedo along with over one hundred more federal agents.
Some were spread out in jeans and blue ATF jackets. Paul
Edgar had his assistant with him, a slim petite female in a blue
skirt and white shirt underneath a blue jacket. She carried a
notebook and pen in her hand. Federal agents found the crate
of guns, the million in cash, and the suitcase filled with the
kilos of cocaine. This was a jackpot for the Feds.

The Mercedes Benz was found with two bodies in the front
seat, which made the girl from the restaurant's credibility
superb. When they brought in the forensic team, they started
covering more ground. Then out the blue, they heard someone
bumping the inside of the trunk. Guns were drawn immediately, and everyone surrounded the Benz.

One of the agents, a tough looking white guy approached
the lock with a small hand held lock buster. He inserted it into
the lock just as whoever was on the inside started beating
against the roof of the trunk again. Three other agents yelled
out, almost in unison. "Put your hands up, DEA, AFT."

The federal agent with the lock buster clicked the trigger.

He heard the click, then opened the trunk. The surrounding agents moved in quickly as the trunk came further open. There was a man inside, on his back, stripped down to his drawers. His hands were cuffed and he was covering his face from the guns and light. He was breathing hard, his chest and stomach, covered with hair, rose and fell with each breath.

Two of the agents put their guns up, reached inside, and pulled him out. He was trembling uncontrollably and there was gash over his left eye, and blood poured down the left side of his face. When they lifted him out, his mouth was taped with a wide strip of duct tape. They stood him up on his feet; he'd peed on himself hours ago and he smelled of staled urine. One of the agents removed the tape from his mouth.

Paul Edgar moved in front of him and looked him square in his eyes. "I'm DEA agent, Paul Edgar. What is your name, sir?"

Pakistan stood there, looking confused, his hands resting in front of him now. He was still cuffed, but he slowly raised his hands and spelled out with his fingers in sign language *I can't speak no English.*

Paul Edgar looked around. "He's deaf. Can anybody do sign language?"

The slim petite female stepped forward and immediately she began using her hands, drawing letters in the air. Pakistan was watching her closely. She asked him his name and he responded with his fingers. "I don't know."

Paul and his assistant looked at each other. Paul then looked at one of the other agents. "Bring the guy in from the restaurant."

The agent turned around and pulled out his radio while walking toward the open garage door. More police cars and detectives were everywhere, and now an ambulance was muscling its way through. The entire scene looked like an episode from CSI. When he got outside, two other officers were removing the man from the backseat of a Denver police car.

Paul took the tall handsome DA's son into the warehouse and brought him face to face with Pakistan. When Pakistan saw him, he immediately played scared and showed pain and fear, trying to back away from him as if he was a demon.

Paul Edgar noticed it all.

Pakistan pointed at him and nodded his head up and down. That only backed up the story the girl was saying back at the restaurant. Without another word, Paul Edgar made a hand gesture, telling them to get him out of there.

This was another major case for him. One that would clearly put him in a better position. At least he thought so.

28

David Steel, Jr. didn't have to go far to be booked. Just a
few blocks away was the Van Cise-Simonet Deten-
tion Center. Paul Edgar took the son of the district
attorney in himself. He was still dressed in his tuxedo, and
David Steel, Jr. walked quietly beside him, his hands cuffed in
front. He really wasn't thinking much about the situation; all he
did was meet a woman online and take her out to dinner. All of
a sudden, this happens. Walking down a long corridor, Paul
Edgar and two Denver homicide detectives led the way to the
booking section of the jail where he was fingerprinted. They
took pictures of him, and after he was processed, they allowed
him to make a phone call.

David walked across the tile floor to the wall facing him
with six pay phones lined up next to one another. Three were
occupied, that left three of them available. He pulled up
between a short, fat black guy with a bald spot in the entire top
of his head, and a medium built white guy who looked drunk
and tired. David Steel the second, grabbed the phone and
punched in his father's number, brought it up to his face and
listened while it rung.

When the groggy voice of his father came on the line, he swallowed, actually feeling the wrath of his situation. It hit him like a sack of rocks.

Instantly, after hearing his father's voice, his eyes teared up. He leaned his arm up against the wall and rested his head against it. "Dad."

"Yes, son?" his father said from the other end.

"I'm in trouble, but it's been some kind of mistake."

"What is it, son?"

"I'm locked up down on Colfax for murder. Apparently, they have the wrong guy." His voice was trembling harder now and tears rolled down his cheeks.

He was clearly caught up in Amil's pink print. Just another pawn.

He was shocked when his father hung up in his face. He frowned. "Hello, Dad. You there?" He panicked and started banging the phone against the wall until it shattered into pieces.

The police rushed him quickly. Paul Edgar was behind the desk signing some paper work when the commotion started. The Denver police had rushed him to the ground before he could get on the opposite side. Paul Edgar could do nothing but shake his head. When they shoved him inside the first available holding tank, all his runts and rage had completely stopped.

Paul Edgar checked his watch. It was getting late. His wife would be sound asleep by now, but he knew she was mad as all outdoors. Paul Edgar met up with two of the local homicide detectives and addressed them both. "The deaf guy, put him in protective custody. We'll transfer him tomorrow." Then he shook both of their hands, turned on his heels and headed home with nothing on his mind but a conviction. It was the son of the head district attorney of Denver, so this would definitely be a high-profile case for him, and he didn't have a clue that Amil was the brain behind this one as well.

FOUR DAYS LATER, Amil was back in Dubai. On this trip, she brought her associate, Cam, with her from Baltimore to let him see another side of the world. Everybody flew in to meet with Amil. Fly, Iris and Smurf all came in and everybody moved and dressed like Muslims. This was only to disguise themselves, just in case the Feds were still watching. They were inside an unknown location where Papa Bear and Falisa were living. Everything was made of marble, stone and gold. Each room featured wide and spacious high vaulted ceilings.

Falisa and Papa Bear occupied the two chairs at each end of the long marble table; both of them were comfortably dressed. They were living in hiding for now, and they weren't going outside anywhere until things got situated with Amil's plan to reverse the game on the Feds and get them off their backs.

Fly was dressed in a cool linen suit, with over forty karats of sparkling diamonds hanging around his neck. Smurf was in linen pants and a fitted tank top he'd gotten from London. He wore Versace shoes and no socks.

Amil had Cam with her like they were on a date. Cam was cool, and she made sure he had himself a couple of bank accounts and was definitely in a better position. Amil introduced him around the table to everybody.

Fly examined him from head to toe. He'd already heard about him from Amil, but this was his first time meeting him. Fly shook his hand and held it, just like how he was holding his eye contact.

"What up brah, I'm Cam." he said to Fly. Amil stood next to him, waiting for her brother to respond.

Fly smiled, his veneers gave him a movie star look. "They call me Fly, we'll talk later."

Moving on around the table, he met Smurf, Iris, Papa Bear and Falisa. Everybody exchanged warm smiles and greetings.

When they were all seated, a line of servants came out, four women, all of them carrying a platter of food and an array of drinks. Falisa took notice of Amil's actions immediately; she knew she'd fallen for the guy, Cam, and she didn't mind it at all. She enjoyed her daughter's actions. They was amusing.

After they ate and talked, Amil, Papa Bear and Falisa all went into a secluded room that was covered with thick lavender carpet, expensive leather sofas and chairs, with the walls painted a soft peach with no windows. Papa Bear and Falisa sat next to each other.

Amil occupied a comfortable leather chair across from them. She kicked her feet up on the ottoman and said, "We got Pakistan inside. We also got the head district attorney's son for a trumped up charge that won't stick unless I make it stick. David Steel has a lot of clout in Denver, and I'll need him on my side in the future."

Papa Bear listened intently, watching the excitement glisten in her eyes. Then he said, "You're real excited, I see."

"Very." She responded, nearly smiling. "Everybody's got a position on this. The main thing is Paul Edgar. He's our pawn. He's the one that's gonna clear up our family name."

"What the time frame looking like, Amil?" Falisa asked. Her eyes fixed on her daughter.

"Two years max, Mother. The pink print is definitely official, and after that, no more hiding."

"And Cam?" Falisa asked.

"Just a business associate. He's never been any further than Baltimore and Washington DC, so I decided to bring him along and let him see other parts of the world."

Falisa smiled at Amil. She was good at reading body language, and even more, she definitely knew her own daughter from head to toe. Falisa folded her arm across her chest, then she changed the subject. "Let's talk numbers."

"You said you wanted a billion, Mother. That's the goal. But what good is it if you can't enjoy it?" She paused, then went on. "So I'll make it my business that neither of you will have to sit in a prison cell again. And now my question to you all is, when is it set?"

Falisa's eyebrows bunched together.

Papa Bear's eyes turned to slits a little bit. They were both watching Amil, waiting to see what she was talking about.

"Don't play crazy with me. Y'all know I know that you're going to get married."

Falisa just smiled. Then she responded, "Once we get this situation dealt with."

"Can I be the best woman?" Amil asked.

"There is no such thing." Papa Bear said, his arm went around Falisa's neck.

"It's a first time for everything." Amil said cheerfully.

29

Later that evening, Fly and Smurf and a couple more
Arabian bodyguards took the young Cam out to see
the city of Dubai. They rode around in the rear of the
Maybach, just the three of them, each one casually dressed in
Tom Ford or either Louis Vuitton. Amil had spent a lot of
money on Cam's attire, and tonight he was in a tailor made
pinstripe suit that she'd bought from a boutique in Dubai.
From behind the tinted windows of the Maybach, they couldn't
help but to notice how beautiful the skyline was, it was illuminated like no other skyline in the world.

"So, brah. I don't mean no harm, but what's really good?
How you just pop up outta nowhere, and my sister is breaking
bread with you and introducing you to the family? Smurf fired
up a Cuban cigar while he waited for an answer.

Cam took the cigar, ran it under his nose. It smelled sweet
and fresh. Fly was quiet, dressed in Alexander McQueen, a
champagne glass in his hand, his eyes on Cam also.

"I don't know, she found me," he said and lit his cigar with a
gold lighter. He smiled at them and added, "I'm official,
though."

"Fuckin' with my sistah. You better be." Fly said.

He leaned toward Cam with his fist balled up. Cam made a fist and touched his. For the next few minutes, they rode in silence. Cam was staring up through the sunroof and watching the stunning skyline.

He looked at Fly. "Man, this like a dream come true. My whole family straight because of y'all, and all I wanna do is keep it like that, even if I got to die."

That statement alone that made Smurf and Fly look at him differently. A man that wanted his family to be all right, he couldn't go wrong. Not dealing with them, anyway.

The driver of the Maybach pulled into the parking lot of a club called Mansion Dubai. Now, Mansion Dubai was an exclusive venue, catering to only a posh and elite clientele, comprised of the crème-de-la-crème of Dubai. Foreign and exotic automobiles filled the parking lot. Mansion was the playground for the rich and extravagant. The drive up line for valet was long, and it took their driver nearly fifteen minutes to get up to the entrance. When the Maybach stopped, the rear door opened on the driver side where Smurf was sitting. He was holding a half smoked cigar when he stepped out. The tip of it was still red and blazing.

A security team waited for them there as well, four Arabian men in suits and huge guns in shoulder holsters underneath their jackets. They formed a half circle at the rear door.

Cam came out next. He looked around in pure amazement, taking in the freshest air that he'd ever smelled. He moved around and stood next to Smurf, the heels of his Tom Fords clicking against the asphalt.

Next came Fly. He stepped out like the Last Don, and with a high stature such as his, he didn't have a reason not to. Here was a man who had grown up from the age of twelve to a full grown man in the game. Now here he was all the way on the other side of the globe, still getting money, and still on his throne.

One of the bodyguards carefully closed the Maybach door, and then the three of them were escorted inside the exclusive club. The inside was laid out like a palace, beautiful women were all over the place. The majority of them had long flowing hair and petite bodies. When they got to one of the private lounges just for the three of them, they found seats on the plush leather sofas and chairs. Bottles of champagne came out, followed by cigars and half-naked beautiful women in heels. Cam had never seen anything like it. The only problem they had was that the Arabs didn't have their type of music playing.

Fly had his very own personal bottle of champagne that he casually sipped straight from the mouth. Smurf was across from him, his own bottle in his hand, and Cam was just over-whelmed by the entire scene. You basically had to be a million-aire to even be in this place, and from the looks of it, he assumed he was plugged for real just by being in Fly and Smurf's presence.

Over the next hour, Fly ordered beautiful women just to come into their private lounge and kick it. More cigars and champagne. Then Fly sat up from his relaxed position, his diamonds sparkling underneath the soft lighting. He turned and looked directly at Cam, and said, "You an official lil nigga." He turned up his champagne bottle and swallowed. "We brought you here because we got a proposition for you."

Smurf lit a cigar and looked straight at Cam.

Cam's eyes darted from Fly to Smurf. He noticed that both of them were serious. Figuring that something else was about to come with this, his heartbeat sped up a little. "I'm listening," he said.

Fly cleared his throat, adjusted in his chair. "We got a couple of associates up in New York that we need to locate." His words were low and powerful.

Fly quietly waited for his response.

Smurf looked at him as a cloud of thin smoke enveloped his face. His eyes turned to slits, just thinking about how the New York goons killed his girl and his partner, Pig Man. "We got a couple of locations on these niggas." Smurf said, and then he blew a stream of smoke from his mouth.

"You got a name?" Cam asked.

"Nigga call himself Rolex." Fly said. He paused and read Cam's facial expression to see if he'd ever heard the name before.

Just then, a female was allowed to come up through their line of bodyguards. She was tall and carried a metal briefcase. She brought it directly to Fly. He took it and sat it on the floor next to him. He was moving slow and careful. Then he said to Cam again. "Nigga calls himself Rolex or Lex."

"If possible, we would like him alive. But if it's not possible, I want him killed one hundred times." Smurf delivered his words with pure hatred. Thinking about how January and Pig Man was killed nearly brought tears to his eyes.

Cam noticed the emotion in his voice, saw the deadly stare in his eyes as well, and that told him a lot. Between Smurf and Fly, he could tell that they were killers, just like him.

"We got a small bonus of five million for you. The cash is here," Fly said, "but you can't take it back to the States in cash, so we gonna set you up an offshore account under one condition."

"And what's that?" Cam asked.

"My sister cannot know anything about this. We just wanna keep it under the table. Is that understood?"

Cam nodded in a slow rhythm while looking Fly dead in his eyes and realizing that he was serious. He was telling them that it wouldn't go any further, and he meant it.

30

W hen Smurf and Fly brought Cam back to the hidden palace, Amil was up waiting for them. It was three thirty A.M., the temperature had dropped a little and a light breeze came through the balcony doors of her bedroom. When Cam walked into her room, the lights were off, but scented candles dimly lit the room. A light vanilla scent rushed his nostrils. She was laying in the bed, her hair down, she looked like an angel glowing against the off-white pillowcase. There was a forty-inch flat screen at the foot of the bed, giving off a soft blue glow through the bedroom.

Cam went to the side of the bed and stood there.

Amil looked over at him, her eyes traveling up and down his body. His eyes were low and red. "You look tired," she said, and then added, "You been out with my brothers, I see."

Cam nodded, then he sat down on the bed.

Amil turned over on her side. She was dressed in a satin two-piece pajama set. Now facing him, she watched his back while he kicked off his shoes. Amil scooted over closer to him, put her hand on his neck, and pulled him back toward her. It was only a small crush that Amil had on him.

Cam leaned all the way back, the scent of champagne seeping off his breath. Amil removed his platinum chain that was flooded with high quality diamonds and slipped it around her neck. She looked down at the sparkling diamonds that rested against her black satin pajama shirt.

Cam turned and faced her. She looked soft and delicate as she reached up and rubbed the side of his face. He seemed worried about something.

"What's wrong?" she asked him.

Cam moved up into the bed and laid next to her. His chest pressing against her breast, he said in a low tone, "I'm loyal to you, Amil, first before anybody else. But I gave yo' brother my word that I wouldn't tell you about this."

Amil's facial expression turned cold and serious. "About what?" Her eyes narrowed.

Cam swallowed. Amil was making him nervous now, and that was not good. He cleared his throat and looked like he was ready to say something, but he couldn't find his words. He took a deep breath and said, "They want me to take a hit on some New York nigga name Rolex. Now I don't have a problem with doing it, but I wasn't comfortable with the part about not saying anything to you about it."

Amil masked her smile with a look of fury on her face. She leaned in and kissed his lips, then she tongued him and tasted nothing but cigars and champagne. She pulled away from him. "Loyalty over everything, baby." She then climbed over him and got out the bed.

He grabbed her hand and squeezed it. "Where you going?"

"To speak with my brothers." She reached down between his legs and slowly squeezed his dick. That shocked him. "Five minutes, and I'll be back for that." Then she turned and left the room.

Amil closed the door behind her, moved down the wide marble corridor, and walked into a room on the left side. The room was spacious and decked out with lavender carpet. A huge marble top bar, two billiards tables, and a bunch of leather chairs and sofas that was set up in different configurations decorated the room. Fly, Smurf, and Iris were all sitting around with their own personal money counting machines and stacks of one hundred dollar bills. All three of them looked up at her at the same time. Her face was still and unreadable.

When she got within a foot of all three of them, her face turned into a smile and she said, "He's official."

Fly smiled and wiped away some imaginary sweat in a joking manner. "Damn! You scared me, girl."

"Me too." Smurf said and smiled.

Amil saluted them. "We good. I'm going to get some rest. I'm flying out first thing in the morning."

Fly stood up, then waved her over to him. She walked over and he hugged her, then kissed her cheek. "Be careful, okay."

"I will, I promise." She shot back.

Smurf stood up, hugged her, and kissed her cheek. "Failure is not an option, baby girl."

Next came Iris. As soon as they embraced, Iris' eyes turned moist. "You sure you don't want me to go with you?"

Amil smiled. "I'm good, darling." Then Amil kissed her cheek, they held on to one another and then separated. Before Amil left, she said, "Just make sure Cam is taken care of."

When she got back to her bedroom, Cam was laying in the bed still dressed. Amil locked the door behind her and started removing her pajama shirt. Her breasts were perky and her nipples were already turning hard. When she got to the bed, Cam sat up.

He stared at her tight body as she loosened the waistband of her pajama pants and carefully worked them down to her ankles. Amil seemed to be nervous as she slowly stepped out of them, one foot at a time; avoiding contact with Cam's piercing eyes.

Cam bit his bottom lip as he took in Amil's lush curves. He couldn't wait to touch her. He moved to the edge of the bed and held his hand out. She walked over and stood between his legs. Cam placed his hands on each side of her waist and pressed his face against her chest. He could feel her heart rate increase as he slowly drew one of her eraser sized nipples into his mouth. Amil let out a little whimper as his tongue caressed her nipple while his hand fondled her other breast.

He pulled her down on the bed next to him and laid her flat on her back. Amil gasped as he kissed a trail down her body, starting with her lips and stopping at her inner thighs. She grabbed a pillow to mask her moans when Cam lightly bit the top of her thigh. Her juices flowed as his breath tickled her lower lips.

Cam raised his head and looked into her eyes, then with a devilish grin, he stuck his index finger into her swollen opening. His eyes never left her face as he explored her body. The way she writhed and moaned from his touch made Cam feel powerful, as if they were equals in that moment. He lowered his head and drew her stiff clit into his mouth. As he gently sucked it, he made a beckoning motion with his finger, stimulating her G spot.

"Oh my God, oh my God, oh my God, oh my God," Amil said breathlessly as the overwhelming sensations washed over her.

"Shh, I got you."

Cam pulled his saturated finger out of her and replaced it with his tongue. He thumbed her clit as he fucked her every wall with his mouth. Amil started to buck under him as if she was having a seizure. Cam simply applied more pressure.

Amil felt like she was climbing the walls. She had lost control of her body and she felt as if she was on a paddleboat heading over a cliff. Involuntarily, her thighs tightened around Cam's head as she came right in his mouth.

The room was silent, only the sound of heavy breathing pierced the air. Amil lay curled in the fetal position, trying to collect herself. She had never came so powerfully before, now, all she wanted was to do it again. Cam was more than ready to oblige. He got completely naked and sat on the side of the bed. She smiled at him in anticipation.

Cam was younger than her by a year, but he was hung and gifted. He smiled at her as he reached into his discarded pants and pulled a lambskin condom out and opened it.

Amil reached over and took the condom from him. Her small hands softly caressed him as she slid it onto his pole. She then laid back and spread her legs, slowly touching herself as he moved over her. With moist fingers, she grabbed his dick and scooted down a little for a better position. She brought the head to her vagina lips and eased him inside of her. She closed her eyes for a brief moment then allowed them to pop open again. Cam pushed himself all the way inside her and she moaned and dug her nails in his shoulders and wrapped her strong muscular legs around his waist.

"Shit." She said through clenched teeth and rotated her hips to meet his thrusts.

Cam tried to pace himself and take his time, but as soon as Amil's warm pussy hugged his dick, he was gone. He was rough and wild; long deep strokes pounding into her depths. Amil was so wet, her lily made a suctioning sound with each stroke. He was working her over. She felt herself about to come again, so she tried to make him slow down, but Cam was too far in. He went deeper with force, sweat poured from his face.

He flipped her over on her stomach and pushed her ass cheeks apart. With one hand on her waist, and the other on her back, he plunged back into her depths.

After the initial shock, Amil was into it. She looked back over her shoulder at him seductively, and met him thrust for thrust. The sound of skin hitting skin filled the room as they enjoyed each other. Amil had the sheets in her mouth to keep from screaming. *Oh my God,* she said to herself.

Cam was about to come, she could feel his pace increase and him expanding inside of her. He let out a loud grunt and then exploded.

Amil laid flat down on her stomach; Cam collapsed on top of her with his nine-inch log still in her. He nibbled on her earlobe and whispered, "I don't ever wanna be without you."

Amil turned her head to the side, then he kissed her lips. He noticed that she had tears in her eyes.

"I never had it like this before," she whispered.

Then they went at it again. And again. And again.

31

W hen Paul Edgar finally got a chance to interview Pakistan, it wasn't as easy as he thought it would be. Inside a small four-corner room at a federal holding facility in Denver Colorado, there was Paul Edgar and his female assistant. She was a specialist in psychology and interrogations. There was a high-tech camera in the upper right hand corner. Pakistan had a worried look on his face and his hair was a mess. He leaned his chair back on its two rear legs while smoking on a Camel cigarette. He didn't smoke for real, maybe a cigar every now and then, but the cigarettes were all part of his act.

A knock came from the door, but whoever it was didn't wait for anyone to tell them to enter. Two other agents came in; they looked cheerful and carried briefcases in one hand and cups of coffee in the other. Pakistan cut his eyes up at them when they walked in, and put his chair back down on all fours. He took a deep breath and looked straight ahead. His gaze wasn't on anyone in particular, he just looked spaced out. His hand rested on the table with the lit cigarette pressed between his two fingers.

One of the two federal agents who had just entered, placed his coffee down on the table, and then his briefcase. Not one word was said between them. The agent opened the briefcase, removed a pair of white latex gloves, and stuffed his fingers and hands inside. Then he pulled out a syringe and tore it from the see through plastic. He turned and looked at Pakistan while pulling out a small glass bottle of truth serum.

Paul Edgar looked at Pakistan; he was anticipating the interrogation after he was injected with the truth serum. Paul Edgar watched as his assistant wiped the inside elbow of Pakistan's left arm with a small alcohol pad. When she was finished, the other agent carefully stepped up and inserted the tip of the needle into Pakistan vein. Pakistan felt the small sting first, and then he looked down at the agent's hand as he pushed the fluid into his vein.

A moment later, he stepped back, watched Pakistan take a draw from his cigarette again. He tilted his head back, he was feeling relaxed, almost like he was floating. He exhaled the smoke, blew a straight line toward the ceiling. Then he set the cigarette down in the groove of the plastic ashtray.

Paul Edgar slid a small note pad across the table to him along with an ink pen. Mini tape recorders came out, some hand held, and one was sitting on the table right in front of him. Pakistan sat still. He was waiting for the truth serum to take effect, and honestly, it was already flowing through his system. His eyes darted around the room to each of the agents. Then he heard a finger snap that came from somewhere and it appeared that he went into a trance.

The first question Paul Edgar wrote on the paper was, *How did you lose your hearing?*

Pakistan read it, his eyebrows bunched together, his eyes came up from the paper in front of him and he looked at each of them one at a time. He then picked up the pen and wrote on the paper in Arabic language: Sometimes I'm completely deaf, but I always hear the wind blowing.

Paul Edgar pulled the small note pad to him and spun it around so he could read it. Paul flashed him a halfhearted smile, then he wrote down on the paper, *Tell us about the double murder. The crate of guns. The money. The cocaine, and the why you were in the trunk.* He slid the note pad back to him.

Pakistan read the note. He figured they'd start there with the questions. Pakistan looked over it, read it repeatedly for five minutes while the agents waited for him to write. The smell of coffee rose in his nostrils, then out of the blue, he parted his lips, and with perfect English, he whispered, "I don't know the names of the people I work for."

Paul Edgar scooted his chair up closer to the table. He was looking more interested now. "So you can hear?" he said. "That means you told a lie from the beginning."

"No, that means I was scared for my life. You can't talk around these people. Even if they're dead."

Small laughs floated around the inside of the interrogation room. Then Paul Edgar said, "I want you to take a polygraph test. Will you cooperate with me on this?"

"I'm being truthful as possible," he said, "but if you want me to take the test, I will." His English was perfect and slow. He looked around the room at the faces of the agents. They were all looking at him.

Paul Edgar cut his eyes up at one of the other agents that came in with the briefcase. He caught the look and immediately took out a lie detector machine. In less than ten minutes, they had Pakistan hooked up, wires running from the tip of his fingers and a monitor machine. Paul Edgar was satisfied now. Between the truth serum and the machine, he knew that there was no way he could get past telling the truth.

"First question, what's your name?" Paul Edgar asked him in the most comfortable tone of voice.

The question registered in Pakistan's head. He took a deep breath and said, "Pakistan. That's all I remember."

Everybody listened carefully, and then their eyes went to the machine to watch how the needles moved. Paul Edgar's eyes went back to Pakistan. He watched him carefully. He knew he'd already told a lie about being deaf, and he knew Pakistan wasn't his real name.

This time, Paul Edgar took a deep breath, leaned up, and eased his elbows on the table. "Tell us, how did you get in the trunk of the Mercedes."

Pakistan stared blankly. He was allowing himself to relax, to focus more on the question. Ten seconds went by. Amil popped up in his head. Fifteen seconds, he heard Amil's voice. "Their lie detector machines are not effective to someone who knows how to stay focused."

"The trunk." Pakistan finally said. "I was in the trunk. They was gonna take me somewhere to kill me."

"Who are they?" Paul Edgar asked him, then his eyes cut to the digital monitor. The room was in total silence. The only sound that could be heard was the light humming from the air conditioner. Then Pakistan said loud and clear, "They are the feds. But I can't say anything more or my whole family will be murdered."

Tension hit the air immediately. The other federal agents in the room were looking anxious and eager now.

"Give me a name, you got to have a name of somebody."

"It's you, Paul Edgar," he said.

That came as a shock to the rest of the agents in the interrogation room. Everybody was looking at him, then they shifted and looked at the moving paper. It read that he was telling the truth.

32

W hen Amil's private jet landed in New York, Cam was waiting for her in the rear of a stretch limousine. As usual, her public attire was the traditional Muslim garb. Her head and lower half of her face was covered. She was traveling alone this evening, because she knew once she was with Cam, she would be well protected. She was supposed to be in Denver tending to the other situation with Pakistan, but she'd allowed her emotions to get in the way of business.

Cam stood outside at the rear of the limousine. He was dressed in an expensive two-piece and Tom Fords that she'd picked out for him. When she got to where he was standing, he hugged her, kissed the side of her face and escorted her to the inside. He got in behind her and closed the door. Cam wore Jean Paul Gautier cologne and the soft scent filled the rear of the limousine when they settled inside.

Amil removed her face and head wrap while the driver of the limousine pulled off across the private asphalt top.

Cam looked over at her and said, "I thought you had some business to handle."

Amil leaned over toward him and rubbed her hand over his head. He wore his hair cut low, her hand was soft and delicate, and cool across his head. "I just wanted to see you," she told him.

Cam kissed her hand and held on to it.

Amil started stripping herself naked. In her mind, she knew had only a couple of hours to fuck up. When she was completely naked, she moved closer to Cam and began undressing him until he was completely naked. Amil couldn't help herself, she'd turned into a sex maniac, and the only person she wanted was Cam. All business was set to the side for the moment. No discussion about the drug shipments. No discussions about money being shipped. No discussions about handling the business.

Amil climbed on his lap and worked herself down on his long and hard dick. She felt herself spreading. Cam sucked on her pretty nipples and hooked his arms under hers. She eased down, her pussy taking every inch that he had to offer. Her hand went around his neck and her breathing started to get heavy. She kissed Cam on his lips with her back arched. "Oh, I really think I'm falling in love with you." she whispered.

Cam was growing harder and longer, and every time he moved his waist and pushed himself further inside of her, she moaned.

Amil buried her face in the groove of his neck, her heart was thumping and her breathing was erratic. She pulled herself back, then looked down. She wanted to see his dick, glossy and shiny, easing in and out of her. That sight alone sent her hormones into overdrive. She finally came, then she raised up off of him, eased down between his onto her knees and buried her face between his legs. Her mouth covered the head of his dick and she slowly sucked it, adding pressure as she took more of him in. She loved his width, his thickness, the way he tasted in her mouth. Amil was indeed a freak on the low, and she was giving Cam her entire freak.

No more than an hour later, they were back at the private airstrip. Her jet was waiting and the pilots had refueled. They left one another with a hug and a kiss, and then she was back on her jet and gone.

On Amil's private jet, she had her own private walk-in shower that was trimmed in marble and gold. She was naked, but her hair was covered with a shower cap. Underneath the water, she massaged herself and slowly turned around and allowed the spray of water to beat softly against her body. Amil had a lot on her plate. Her plot with the federal agent was official, but she was slowly losing interest, due to the fact that it seemed to her that she had Paul Edgar where she wanted him. With a soft sponge, she traced the length of her left arm. Just that fast, her mind was back on Cam. She was becoming obsessed with him.

Cam's thin sexy body flashed before her eyes. Then she smiled when she envisioned his long thick dick hanging between his legs. Her vision was clear of that, and the thought of it made her touch herself between her legs. Her clit was firm and swollen when she touched it. Cam was behind her, at least she thought of it as a nice feeling anyway. In her mind, he'd bent her over and eased himself all the way up in her. Amil put her left hand against the wall and played with her pussy with the other one. Then when she felt herself about to cum, she squeezed her legs tightly together and yelled, "Get this pussy, baby. It's yours, it's yours. I promise."

Twenty minutes later, she was sitting in a tan leather recliner dressed in a Lululemon jogging suit. She was reclined with her laptop on her lap, chatting online with some poor woman who was fed up with her husband and how his work interfered with their marriage. Amil was posing as a white male with long sandy red curly hair, a muscular-chiseled form with sexy eyes. A California surfer that sold surf boards online, with a simple name: Ken Taylor. He was in his mid-forties and handsomely wealthy. A traveler who was always in and out of the country.

Amil was fascinated with the conversation she was having with the woman. She typed, *My wife is leaving town tomorrow, flying to Canada for the weekend to visit her sister. Is there any way that you can get away? A public place?*

Amil waited, staring blankly at the illuminated blue screen. Seconds passed quickly and the first minute just went. Her stomach tightened a little, a small fear washed over her. Amil took a deep breath. After two minutes, she raked her fingers through her hair and thought to herself, *I lost her.* Then she tossed the computer to the side. Now she was angry, and that wasn't good.

She looked down at the computer screen; a message had just come in. Amil picked up her computer and read the message. *Talk later, he came home.*

"Damn." Amil said.

33

Sarah Edgar closed her laptop when she heard her husband, Paul, pulling up into the driveway. Through the curtains, she saw the headlight of his car dancing across the front and side of the house. She allowed the curtain to fall back into place. Dressed in only a pink see through gown and barefoot, she went back to the bed and eased the laptop underneath her bed into the normal place where she kept it.

Sarah climbed back into bed and pulled the covers up to her neck. She turned over on her side, facing the wall. Her back would be towards the door when Paul came in. She closed her eyes and took a couple of deep breaths to calm herself down.

In her mind, she only thought about Ken Taylor. When she heard her husband's footsteps on the other side of the door, her heart fluttered a little. Sarah hadn't ever cheated on her husband, and didn't plan on doing so, but she did have plans to at least meet Ken Taylor one time.

Paul came through the door and she tried her best to play sleep. She heard him removing his clothes; he was trying his best to keep quiet and not wake her. He hung his keys on a wood hook next to hers and kicked off his shoes. When he climbed into bed, he scooted over next to her and kissed the back of her neck. She moved, then pressed her ass against him.

Paul was tired, as usual. He reached around and cupped her breast; she relaxed to his touch, then all of a sudden he just stopped.

She turned around and faced him. She was disgusted and wanted to know what the problem was. "What is it, honey? What's wrong?" she asked.

Paul looked at her. His eyes were blood shot red and he looked tired for real. He took a long drawn out breath, turned his head towards her, and said in a low tone, "I've been under scrutiny for the last couple weeks since the witness said verbatim that he worked for me. But the good part is that I passed every lie detector test that they have given me. So I'm alright, it's just the pressure of going through all of it."

Sarah kissed him on his cheek and rubbed the side of his face. They stared into each other's eyes for a brief moment.

"So what happened with the witness?" she asked softly.

"I assume he's still in protective custody. I'm off the case now, but I got to be in Washington D.C tomorrow evening for a meeting."

"What is it this time?"

"Another promotion, a better position. Hopefully I don't have to work as much, and we can start spending more family time together.

"Sounds good, honey." Sarah said and moved closer to him.

She was already wet and horny from thinking about Ken Taylor. She reached down between his legs and rubbed his penis, but it didn't budge; it was still soft. That was it. She was fed up. Sarah leaned in, kissed his lips softly and flashed him a smile that had the word artificial written all over it. "Get some rest, honey," she said in a low whisper, the she removed her hand and turned her back to him.

As Sarah lay there, she closed her eyes and imagined how

strong and muscled Ken's body was. She was even more curious now. She wondered what he smelled like. From his pictures, he looked like he could be a good candidate for an after-shave commercial. That thought almost made her smile. Then she wrapped her arms around herself and went to sleep.

The following morning, Paul Edgar was up at seven. Sarah had gotten up an hour earlier and cooked breakfast. Only for herself and him, because the kids were with their grandparents. When he walked into the kitchen, he was fully dressed in navy blue two piece suit, a crisp white shirt and his loose tie was hanging around his neck. He carried a black suit bag on his shoulder.

Paul walked up to Sarah and kissed her lips. "Good morning, I'm in a hurry. Tie me up." He held his head up.

Sarah reached up and tied his tie perfectly. She had been doing it since she was child, after watching her mother do it for her father. After she finished, she smoothed it down and asked, "Do you have time to eat breakfast?"

He shook his head and kissed her lips again. "I really don't." He turned, and as he walked towards the door, he said, "I'll call you when I land in Washington."

Sarah put her hands on her hips and shook her head sadly. She went to the stove and turned the pilot off on the frying pan where she was about to cook turkey bacon and omelets. Sarah walked into the living room, went to the window to see if Paul had left. She knew he was gone, she but wanted to check again for her own purposes.

When she got to her bedroom, the first thing she did was pull out her laptop, bust it open and send Ken Taylor an email from a bogus gmail account she'd set up.

34

Cam was living the good life in New York, running a multi-million dollar empire from a penthouse in downtown Manhattan with six of his best men that he had on his payroll. Six killers, all from Baltimore with impressive track records and street resumes. Word of mouth spread in the streets just like it does for any legitimate business. If your reputation has you credited as a shooter or killer, somebody will probably hire you.

Tonight, Cam was laying out the red carpet for his circle of Goons. According to Amil's instructions, they were all to dress up in expensive attire from head to toe, and go out on the town to wherever the major players in New York hung. Cam had a couple of photos of Rolex, and the one that he'll never forget is the one where he was dressed up in all black with a huge platinum and diamond chain around his neck, and standing next to a blue Bugatti sports car. There was no doubt that Rolex and his New York circle were millionaires. They did it all, sold keys of cocaine and heroin upstate and down south. They did million dollar tax scams. They sold guns to their other New

York homeboys. They sold hot cars, expensive ones at that. But all in all, they were touching millions of dollars just like them.

Around the huge penthouse living room there was an egg yolk colored baby grand piano with gold emblems all over it. Cam walked over to it. He wasn't completely dressed. His lounge gear was a wife beater and Sean John sweat pants. At the piano, he pressed down a couple keys and the sound wafted through the penthouse. When he sat down on the stool, his homeboys all turned around and looked at him as if he was crazy. One of them said, "Damn main man, you playing the white keys. I thought you only sold them."

Cam smiled, then he ran his hand from one end of the piano keys to the other. He stood up and addressed them all. "It feels good to be here." He looked at this watch; time was ticking. "We gonna get dressed, ya'll ready?"

Two of the guys were playing the x-box game on the big screen TV and they were caught up in their own world. Cam lit up a blunt filled with exotic marijuana. Walking around on the cold marbled floor barefooted, he handed one of the guys the blunt and turned around and walked off towards the bedroom. Nearly twenty minutes later, he was dressed.

The phone rang. He turned his head toward the nightstand and answered it. "Hello," he said as he sat down on the bed.

"Hey sweetheart." Amil said from the other end.

Cam blushed a little. "What up, baby?" he said. Amil's voice made him feel some type of way.

"What are you doing?"

"Just got dressed. Me and my team about to go see the big apple."

"I wanna see you."

"When?" he asked curiously. "You know I got my homies up here with me."

"I don't care. You can bring them with you."

"I got to handle this business first, Amil." He said clearly. He didn't want to disappoint her.

She was quiet on the other end, then she finally said in a sad voice, "Well, I guess I understand. Maybe tomorrow then."

Cam stood up and smiled with the phone still pressed against the side of his face. "Cool, tomorrow. And hopefully I can get this other business handled tonight."

"I hope so too. I actually got some business to handle myself. See you tomorrow then."

"Tomorrow, baby." He ended the call and set the cordless phone back inside its tray.

When he walked back to the spacious living room, all his partners were dressed and waiting for him. He looked them all over and was completely satisfied. "Y'all ready?" He asked them all at the same time.

They were already casually dressed since they were only going out to kick it. Every one of them was strapped with fancy handguns, beams and extended clips. Also, they wore thin Kevlar vests underneath their shirts. Tonight they weren't looking for Rolex or no trouble, however if it happened to come to them, they would be prepared. As the old saying goes, it's better to be caught with it than without it.

Downstairs, Cam and his six man team came from the elevator looking like a million dollar team of rappers. They were draped in diamonds, sparkling underneath the soft lobby lighting. Cam led the way through the electronic doors. They walked outside, and everyone filed straight into the rear of a waiting limousine. Night had fallen, and the New York skyline was lit up.

They rode through the streets of Manhattan, and they fit right in because limousines riding downtown was more than normal. In the rear, Cam passed around a box of Columbian cigars. They opened two bottles of Hennessy XO and drank from them in Styrofoam cups.

Then, out of the blue, one of the other guys said, "Main man, since we out and about, what about the forty-forty club?" He was looking at Cam from behind a pair of lavender tinted shades. He held an unlit cigar in one hand and a cup of XO in the other.

"Yeah... That's Jay-Z's spot. You know money niggas hang out up in there."

Cam pulled out a gold lighter and struck it, brought it to the tip of his cigar and lit it. He puffed and then a cloud of smoke enveloped his face. "Forty forty club it is then."

35

In Denver, Colorado, Amil was secure and tucked away inside a two million dollar log cabin in the mountains. She was standing in front of huge stone-faced fireplace watching the logs burn slowly, mesmerized by the burning flames. She held an untraceable smart phone up to her face, listening intently to Falisa on the other end. Amil turned around; high shined wood floors and several pieces of expensive furniture surrounded her. There was a huge white Bearskin rug with the head on it laying on the floor. She walked to it, kicked off her bedroom shoes and sat down on it in Indian style.

"I'm not keeping you in the blind, Mother. Honestly, I'm about to meet the agent's wife. I'll have a talk with her, it'll be simple. Trust me, please." She rubbed her hand across the fur of the rug, her nails were long and painted pink.

Her mother was quiet on the other end. Then Falisa said, "The first sign you get in your gut, trust it. Pull out, and come back to Dubai."

"Yes, Mother," was all she said.

"Keep me updated every three hours. I love you, baby."

"I will, and I love you too, Mother." She ended the call, set the phone down, folded her arm across her lap and closed her eyes. One long deep breath and she began to meditate.

She sat there in the same position for nearly an hour, clearing her thoughts. Her mind was blank and free, to the point that her face was turning into a smile. When she opened her eyes, she stood up to her feet. Then stretched her arms high above her head. She turned, walked across the floor, went to the front door, and opened it.

The air was thin up in the mountains, but it was refreshing when she inhaled. Staring around, she saw a car coming up the road that led to her cabin. Satisfied, she turned around and closed the door. When she went to the bedroom, she immediately dressed up in a maid uniform, then tied the clean crisp white apron around her waist. She went to the mirror, pinned up her hair and wrapped it in a ball, no makeup or nothing. Then she slipped on a pair of cheap looking leather shoes, adjusted her skirt, and by the time she got to the front door, the car was parked in front of the cabin.

Through the front windshield, she could see her associate, a white man from England with sandy red hair. His name was Ken Taylor... for the night at least. He stepped out, ran around to the passenger side door and opened it for Sarah Edgar. She wore a scarf draped over the top of her head and some big block shades that covered her eyes.

Amil watched her associate kiss Sarah when she stepped from the passenger seat of the car. That alone made her smile from ear to ear. Today, she was a simple ass maid who kept the cabin clean for the millionaire, Ken Taylor. When they started coming towards the front of the cabin, Amil politely opened the door for them. Ken Taylor had his hand on the small of Sarah's back and allowed her to step inside first.

When Sarah got to Amil, she smiled and greeted her with a

casual, "Good morning," and bypassed her just like the simple maid that she appeared to be.

Amil smiled at her, then bowed her head. "Morning."

Ken Taylor came in behind Sarah, winked at Amil, and then he said to her, "We'll only be here for one hour."

Amil closed the door behind them and locked it. She turned around and watched Ken Taylor lead Sarah straight to the master bedroom. All she could do was smile at her magnificent plan. Even though it was still at the beginning stages, she knew this part of her pink print was the most crucial.

Inside the huge master bedroom, Ken Taylor took Sarah by the hand, and guided her straight towards the canopy bed. He removed her shades from her eyes and her scarf; her eyes were uneasy.

She stared up at Ken. He was an even six four with a chiseled frame from his neck down to his ankles. "I'm nervous," she whispered.

Ken leaned down and kissed her on her soft pink lips. She closed her eyes and felt her heart flutter. She was wet between her legs, then she felt herself trembling when his hand touched her vagina. "Oh my God." She mumbled. Her eyes popped open. "What about your maid, you think she knows my face?"

"You have nothing to worry about," he said. His voice was charming and very persuasive. "You've trusted me thus far."

She nodded, her eyes turned to slits and she licked her lips. She was hot and horny, with a hunk standing directly in front of her. Ken began undressing her while she tugged and snatched at his belt and pants.

"Please use a condom," she said to him while stepping out of her pants.

～

IN THE NEXT ROOM, Amil watched everything from a flat screen color monitor. She had a state of the art surveillance system setup on a small table. Sarah was naked, her hair was long and her skin was pale with rose colored nipples and a fat pink vagina between her legs. She was sitting at the edge of the bed rolling the condom on Ken's long thick shaft. He was standing dead in front of her.

When she got the condom completely on, she didn't hesitate to deep throat him. Amil smiled, she was impressed. *She's clean,* Amil thought and bit down into the top of a sweet strawberry. Amil then picked up a remote, pressed the volume button to get sound.

"You like this dick already, I see." Ken said while rubbing his hands through her hair.

Sarah looked up at him; her eyes were dreamy. "God, yes."

She leaned back, grabbed his dick with both hands, spread her legs and invited him in.

Ken didn't waste any time. He folded her legs back and took control. When he got inside, he noticed she was tight, very tight, like wet hands squeezing him. That surprised him. Her eyes were begging him to fuck her; she needed it bad because her husband wasn't doing it.

For the next hour, Ken fucked Sarah from every angle and every position, and Amil had it all recorded. She finally got up from her chair, soaking wet between her legs just from watching. She went to the master bedroom door, still dressed like a maid. After she knocked quickly on the door, she heard Ken's voice from the inside. "Come in."

Amil twisted the brass knob and pushed the door open. Ken and Sarah were laying there underneath the sheets. Sarah didn't look surprised when she stepped inside. She was so gone on Ken and how he fucked her, she didn't care about Paul Edgar anymore.

Amil walked up to the bed where they laid. She went to Sarah's side and stood there looking at her.

Ken whispered, "Slide over, let her in."

Sarah moved closer to Ken, while Amil took off her clothes and revealed her flawless body to two complete strangers. Sarah stared at Amil's breasts, tight stomach and muscular legs. Amil then moved the covers back and slid in the bed next to her. Ken put his hand between Sarah's legs. She was sore, but his touch still felt good.

Amil whispered in her ear, "Promise me you'll never say anything to anyone about this."

"Oh, I swear to God, I'll never say anything to anyone about this." She was nervous, but it was more like an adrenaline rush.

Amil touched her hair. "Such pretty hair, pretty pink skin. Pretty pink nipples. Even your pussy is a pretty pink print."

Later that evening, Amil cleaned up the cabin from top to bottom. Ken Taylor, her associate, had taken Sarah back to the destination where they'd met. She was clean, dressed in a two-piece pants suit and Red Bottoms. She wore big diamonds in her earlobes and had all her paperwork and information sealed in a briefcase. Looking like she was ready for the cover of Forbes magazine, she was well on her way. When she got ready to leave, her cellphone rang. She picked it up from the bed and saw that it was Falisa. She pressed the answer button. With a smile on her face, she said, "Hello mother, we got everything situated."

"No we don't. Something happened in New York with Cam and his team. It must be bad, because Fly, Smurf and Iris are headed to New York." Falisa said.

Amil's heart dropped into her stomach. "Nothing happened to him," she said to her mother. Then without thinking rationally, she hung up the phone and headed to New York.

36

I t took Amil nearly four hours to arrive back in New York. She was just there a couple days ago, and now she was getting all kinds of uneasy feelings running through her veins. Her stomach was in knots. From her private jet, she'd made several calls to Cam, but there was never an answer and the calls were going straight to voicemail.

Her jet finally came to a halt and then it moved again, as the pilot guided it into a huge hanger. Amil stood up. Casually dressed from head to toe, she moved down the steps, a body-guard in front of her and another one behind her.

The rear door of the limousine that waited for her was already open and awaiting her arrival. Iris stepped out just as they made it to the bottom of the steps. Her hair was down, hanging straight, and with a designer skull cap pulled down on top of that. She wore a dark pea coat that stopped at her knees. Amil was looking Iris straight in her eyes, and from what she was reading from them, the news was not good.

The first thing they did was embrace, then they kissed each other's cheek. Amil took her hands in hers, then she asked her, "What's wrong? What happened?"

Without a flinch, Iris said, "They caught Cam and his crew, obviously they wasn't prepared. All of them are dead. They burned them up and left them hanging from handcuffs and pipes. They made Cam call Fly, but the guy, Rolex, just wanted to hear Fly's voice. Fly offered five million for his release and was ordered to bring it here personally. So we all came, as one. And by the time we got here, they'd already killed them and told us where to find the bodies."

Amil was stunned. She couldn't believe it. Her heart wasn't ready for this. Cam was like her first love, and she actually wanted to be with him. Her world had crumbled overnight. Her eyes were still on Iris, they were still holding hands. Amil felt like crying, but she fought it and sucked it up like the Queen she was. "What else did they say?"

Iris thought back to what Fly had told her that he said before their last phone call ended. Then she said, "That they were untouchable."

Amil nodded. "Where are Fly and Smurf?"

Iris guided her the rear of the limousine. Once they got inside, her bodyguards loaded up inside a Yukon with big knobby tires and tinted windows.

Iris looked at Amil and said, "Fly and Smurf got word that the dude Rolex is the head of the crew up here that calls themselves the Picasso Money Gang."

Amil listened intently. Her mind was twisting and turning in every direction. She thought about her associate, Pakistan, who was on the inside and couldn't do anything until she got around to handling that task. Then Paul Edgar and his wife, Sarah. But this new situation with Cam had made everything shift in another direction. Her eyes went to Iris. "The Picasso Money Gang, huh?" She turned and stared out the tinted window as the limousine was pulled out of the hangers and cruised across the asphalt flat top.

"Fly and Smurf are setting up." Iris said while pulling out

her untraceable cellphone. She punched a number and it went straight to Fly. His voice came through from the other end. "She just made it in."

"Alright. You know where we at."

Iris ended the call; her eyes were glued to Amil. She could imagine her pain, she'd already felt the wrath in the past from the successful hit that was put on them. Amil turned her head, her eyes were caught up in Iris' eyes. Their stare was calm but with an evil ferocity. Amil knew that Iris was a professional killer. She was skilled and knew weaponry like the back of her hand, but she was bothered by something, and that something was, *why didn't Papa Bear come?* Even though she knew he had to stay there to protect her mother, she still felt that he should've come to assist her. That was Amil though, she pushed the thought to the back of her mind and folded her arms across her chest.

"What bout Papa... He's still in Dubai, correct?"

That made Iris smile. Flashing a commercial ready set of teeth, she shook her head and said, "Papa came to the States two days earlier he went straight to North Carolina. He found Rolex family down there and got all the information we needed to locate Rolex."

"Have all their bodies been disposed of?"

"Yes, everything has been handled and he was back in Dubai in time for breakfast with the queen."

That made Amil smile from ear to ear, just hearing about Papa Bear coming in to aid her. The situation made him just that much more respected, and now it was her turn to return the favor to her family. Bottom line, she didn't want her family running anymore. She took a deep breath. "We need to get this New York situation situated. ASAP."

"I agree," Iris said. "But the only information Papa got out of his family was a phone number to a studio and the address."

"Well fine, setup a surveillance team at the studio. Somebody gonna show up eventually.

WHEN AMIL and Iris arrived at the penthouse where Smurf and Fly were posted, it was nearly an hour and twenty minutes later. The traffic was thick and congested. Amil went straight to the wet bar once she got inside; Iris was right behind her. Fly and Smurf and two more foreign looking gentlemen all sat around on fine leather furniture. Amil didn't say one word to either of them until after she poured herself a half filled glass of champagne.

From across the room, she asked, "What's your take on the situation? Anybody."

Fly spoke up first, but not before he stood up, bracing himself on an oak wood cane. He faced her. "These niggas was flexin'. They went to the forty forty club and saw these niggas from New York that didn't have nothing do with nothing. Cam and his crew sent over twelve bottles of champagne with a red rose in each bottle. Trying to be sarcastic, I guess. But nothing was said after that. From my understanding, the New York crew told them thank you and actually drank the champagne. They they ambushed them once they were outside." He paused and looked at Iris and asked her, "Did you fill her in on the rest?"

Iris nodded.

Amil sipped from her glass, her eyes still on Fly. "So what's the hold up now?" she asked. "Cause I got this business to handle."

Fly nodded, nothing else was said.

37

A week later, at almost seven A.M., there was a thick blanket of fog moving through downtown Manhattan like one large ghost. High beam head-lights from the many different automobiles made the scene look even more uneasy. This morning, Amil and Iris worked as a team, dressed in clean, but shabby Muslim women garb with Nike jogging suits underneath and black running sneakers, just in case they had to leave on feet. However, they looked plain, simple and harmless. In front of them was a blue van parked on the curb just in front of Rolex's studio.

Amil's face was covered from her mouth down, leaving her nose and eyes and forehead exposed. Iris was the same way. They both hopped in the van through the side door. A long fold-out table leaned against the wall of the van. Iris got one end, and Amil got the other end.

They exited the van with the table, unfolded the legs, and set it up right there on the sidewalk in front of the studio. Amil went and got a tablecloth and draped it over the table. The front face of the studio was built out of gray stone and had automatic glass doors. Their table was no more than ten feet away from the doors. The high-rise building was surrounded by more high rises, making the area shady and cold. Today was their first day on this mission, and they were only rolling the dice, not knowing if Rolex would show up today or not. But they'd made up in their mind that they weren't leaving New York until they got who they came for, and that was Rolex and his so called Picasso Money Gang.

Next, they pulled two small cardboard boxes from the van. The boxes were filled with an assortment of oils in miniature bottles for men and women both. They also had scented candles and soaps, fruit and other necessities.

They had their own personal handguns, which looked like something that Trinity and Naomi had on the Matrix movie, and beyond that, they were both wearing a side weapon underneath their clothes with bullets that could press straight through a Kevlar vest.

Just across the street, Fly was behind the wheel of yet another type of service van. He was cool, and wore a fake gray beard wrapped around his face. He watched the studio from the window, while Smurf occupied the rear of the van with a high caliber machine gun that hung from a hook in the ceiling of the van, suspended by a chain. There was a string of fifty caliber bullets with over one thousand rounds feeding through the gun. From where the van was parked, if the rear double doors were open or either the side sliding door, Smurf would have a clean shot on whatever got in his way. Hopefully, he wouldn't have to use it, and Iris and Amil could handle it before he'd have to let the beast go that he was sitting behind.

Back on the street, two more women approached Iris and Amil. They were dressed the same way, and they appeared to be customers. The women pulled out a hand full of cash and bought oils and fruit. They gave Amil a nod, letting her know that they were out there with her.

Amil and Iris stood next to each other on the back end of

the table. They smiled, and the two women turned and walked off. The perfect picture was painted for their decoy, and now they would wait them out.

After five hours, the fog had lifted and there still wasn't any sign of Rolex, and as a matter of fact, nobody had come into the building that matched the description that they had in mind. They'd sold several bottles of oils and a few scented candles, standing on their feet, waiting and watching.

Amil pushed her sleeve up and looked at her watch. She needed to get to Denver, and it was mandatory that she get there very soon. She looked at Iris. "I gotta leave, and I probably won't be back until tomorrow afternoon," she said to her. "Can ya'll handle everything until I get back?"

Iris gave her a strong and confident stare and followed with a head nod. She leaned over and hugged Amil. "Hurry back, we just getting comfortable."

Amil left on foot. She turned a couple of blocks where a yellow cab waited. Another Arabian looking man was waiting patiently behind the wheel. Amil bounced into the backseat and the driver started the engine. After a few more blocks, Amil was dropped off at a waiting limousine in a parking garage somewhere in Queens. Then, within another thirty minutes, the limousine was pulling into the parking lot of the private airstrip where her pilots waited for her on her Gulfstream G5.

When she got on her jet, the first thing she did was strip naked and get into the shower. Her body was tired, and even aching in some areas. She needed some rest, but that would have to come later.

After she showered and dressed, she pulled out her laptop, sent her friend, Sarah Edgar, a message, and waited for a response. Two minutes later, the words from Sarah Edgar rolled across her computer screen. *It was kind of complicated, but I got it.*

Amil typed back, *I'm in route to you now. Can u meet me at the cabin? My time is limited and the doctors are there waiting for you and I.*

She waited for a response while rubbing her hands together.

Then Sarah Edgar's message came across her screen. *I'll be there.*

Amil smiled from ear to ear, her heart thumping inside her chest. What she was about to do would either put her in position or behind bars for the rest of her life.

38

The following afternoon, Amil was on her jet, headed back to New York. On her flight back, she was quiet and her stomach was flipping in knots. The doctors told her that she would probably sweat or feel nauseated, but other than that, everything was all right. She tried to get some shuteye, but she couldn't. Her adrenaline was running on overload. A sharp pain raced through her body, she cringed and her face balled up. It felt as if she was about to vomit, but it didn't come all the way up. Still the nasty acid taste was in her throat.

By the time her jet landed, she'd gotten herself together and was feeling a little better, and taking the same route back. She took the limousine to the cab and the cab back downtown, and then she was back on foot again. Walking across the street from the studio, she saw Iris as she was just the day before, still standing behind the table hustling bottles of oil, and incognito to whoever came in her presence. Amil saw Fly behind the wheel of the van, this time it was beige. They would change colors every day if it would keep them a few steps ahead of the game. Cars passed by, some horns were honking from a distance. Amil walked up further and then crossed the street

directly in front of the van. She walked right past Fly and
Smurf and acted as if she didn't know them.

When she got to Iris, they embraced, and Iris asked her,
"Did everything go alright?"

"It did," she said cheerfully and nodded. Then she turned
around and faced the street, got right back into the groove of
things as if she hadn't missed a beat.

For almost three weeks, they repeated this routine daily,
with no sign of Rolex or his crew. Finally, on the twenty-first
day, they the tide changed.

A LIGHT WIND was blowing and Amil caught a chill and shiv-
ered. She wasn't feeling her best, but she was determined to see
this through. In that moment, Cam flashed before her eyes. It
was a vision of him and it was still hard for her to believe that
he was dead. She shook her head and tried her best to push the
thought from her mind. His face reminded her of her mission
and purpose for why she was standing downtown in the middle
of New York City. They had taken what was hers, and no one
takes from Amil. Ever.

Loud motorcycle engines came roaring down the street.
Amil turned her head to the left and so did Iris. To their
surprise, twin Ninja motorcycles, shiny black and riding side by
side pulled up. Their headlights were on, even though it was
broad daylight. Just behind them was four dark colored
Bugattis riding back to back with their headlights on also. The
entourage was heading straight for Amil and Iris. They pulled
up fast, revving the engines on the expensive million dollar car.

Amil immediately grabbed a couple bottles of oil and Iris
picked up a couple of candles. Traffic was thick. Pedestrians
were coming and going. Amil walked up to the curb. She
wanted a closer look inside to see if one of those faces belonged

to Rolex, but just then, the passenger side door opened on all four Bugattis in unison. Big black guys dressed in black made her stop in her tracks.

"Step back," the guy said. He looked past her and saw the table set up and then looked back at Amil. "Who the fuck tole ya'll bitches to set up shop on this corner?"

Within a split second, Amil's eyes searched the line of Bugattis and saw Rolex's face. He was sitting behind the wheel of the third car. She didn't need to see any more. She gave Fly a signal by touching her left earlobe. Then, Amil and Iris separated and walked off, leaving the crew right there. Out of nowhere, a man in raggedy clothing ran up to the two guys on the motorcycle, aimed a Berretta at their heads and squeezed the trigger.

Inside the van, Fly saw Amil give him he the signal but he couldn't whip the service van around in time. He looked back at Smurf. "We got action." He said while pulling the van up next to where all four of the Bugattis were parked.

Smurf flipped the latch on the side door and pushed it open. Then he got back behind the fifty-caliber machine gun. He took aim, and before he squeezed the trigger, he whispered, "Georgia, nigga.".

Rolex was just now trying to reach for whatever type of side arm he had, but it was entirely too late for that. When Smurf got on the trigger, nearly fifty rounds burst from the barrel. The huge bullets were ripping and tearing through the glass and the body of the Bugattis. The gun was whistling and the shells were clinking against the inside of the van. Smurf rotated the large caliber machine gun back and forth, hitting each car.

The gun was so loud, he couldn't hear Fly screaming at him. Smurf was zoned out. His face was angry and his heart was aching. Some of the bodies had been ripped from their limbs. Fly was pulling the van from the scene and that's when Smurf finally let up off the trigger. The entire van smelled like oil and gun powder. Smurf managed to get around and tried closing the door. He stumbled, when Fly made a sharp turn.

Then out of nowhere, several agents began spilling out into the street. Cars were closing in. Iris rolled into the front passenger seat and closed the door behind her. She looked at Fly. "Pull off. Just go easy," was all she said."

Fly didn't exchange another word. His eyes darted between the front window and the rearview mirror. As they pulled off, he saw his little sister in the mirror, her hands high above her head. The further he got, all he could do was shake his head in disgust.

Damn! He slammed his hand into the steering wheel.

39

After several hours had passed, Amil was finally fingerprinted and placed into custody in a federal holding facility in lower Manhattan. It was almost three o'clock in the morning, and she was tired as shit to the point that her legs were like rubber and her eyes were barely able to stay open. They locked her inside a four-corner room with clean white walls and a high ceiling with no tables, no chairs, just a cold linoleum tile floor. The air conditioner blew from two vents, one high above the door and the other one aiming directly at her feet.

Amil went to the far corner, wrapped her arms around herself, and slid down the wall. She drew her knees up into her stomach and faced the door that didn't have an inside door knob. Amil wrapped her arms around her knees, dropped her head in her lap, and closed her eyes for only what seemed like five minutes, but in reality, it was three straight hours. When she woke up, there were two federal agents standing over her, a tall handsome male and an attractive female, both casually dressed and well mannered.

"Good morning, Miss. Walker." the female agent said to Amil.

Amil raised her head, and when she opened her eyes, she used her hand to shield them from the light. After a quick moment to get her bearings, Amil bounced up on her feet and shook off her sleep. She was ready for whatever they had to offer her. Then, without any warning whatsoever, vomit erupted from her mouth and hit the pants legs and shoes of the male agent. Her face was twisted and there was the nastiest taste in her mouth. She gagged, then she threw up again.

Twenty minutes later, they escorted Amil to the nurses' station. After they'd run several tests on her, they informed her that she was pregnant. From the looks of it, that definitely came as a shock. Afterwards, they escorted her back upstairs in hand-cuffs, this time they took her to a state-of-the art interrogation room that was surrounded with four walls of mirror glass. A round wooden table sat in the center of the room with four leather swivel chairs. Amil took a seat and they left her in there alone. Her hair was a mess, she observed as she looked around at the glass mirrors that surrounded her.

Cameras were in each corner. She knew they were watching her from behind the one sided glass. She put her elbows on the table, her hands propped underneath her chin, and while staring into space, she began having doubts about the whole situation. For one, she wasn't supposed to be there. Not today, her plan was to turn herself in with the right legal team backing her as the mouthpiece. But instead, she'd been caught at the scene of a crime where at least eight people had been murdered. The best part about it all, is that she didn't murder anyone, and she didn't have a weapon on her when she was caught.

The door of the interrogation room opened and four federal agents, two men carrying briefcases and two women with leather file folders walked in. They all walked straight to the high polished circular table and began opening folders and briefcases, and flashing their badges. A polygraph machine was produced and hooked up to Amil. They strapped up her fingers and made her sit with her right hand flat down on the table.

Amil relaxed herself by taking a couple of deep breaths. Her head and eyes were fixed straight forward. She stared at the glass. Although she couldn't see anyone on the other side, she knew they were watching her. Still, she remained calm. This one was for the money. For the family. For the Throne.

Amil began to think about flowers, pretty Tulips, red roses, and a wide field of beautiful flowers. She was tricking herself, training her thoughts to see everything that relaxed her. Her eyes closed, she thought about her Yoga and Pilates instructor, things that mattered to her in that moment.

The four agents set up tape recorders, even though the entire room was equipped with listening devices that could nearly hear a mouse piss on cotton. They still were not leaving any loose ends. The first lady's name was Emily Tucker; she had black hair and a fair face with a petite body. She sat down in front of Amil with a file opened in front of her. She cleared her throat while looking at Amil.

Amil heard it and opened her eyes. Without them asking any questions, Amil started in a soft voice, being very careful how she chose her words. "My name is Amil Walker, the daughter of Timothy Timbo Walker. At the age of nine years old, my father told that he needed me to become a federal agent and that my brother needed to be able to know the entire drug trade at ten." She paused; her eyes were open and staring into Emily's eyes.

The other three agents looked at the sensors and the paper from the polygraph machine. So far, it appeared that she was telling the truth.

Amil went on. "My father was born in New York City. He was smart, and graduated from high school at the age of sixteen. By the time he'd completed his first year in college, he met a man who later became his best friend. Paul Edgar was his name. This same man, Paul Edgar, and my father came up with a magnificent idea that my father would become this big kingpin drug dealer, and he, Mr. Paul Edgar, was gonna be a federal DEA agent." Amil got quiet again after that statement. Every agent in the room looked at one another, then they looked at the machine again... and again, it appeared that she was telling the truth.

She took another breath. She knew she was lying, but they were going for it, and it was looking damn good, according to their machine. This time, she closed her eyes before speaking. "Mr. Paul Edgar was twenty one years old when he went to his basic training course in Quantico, Virginia. It was on the exact date of October eighth, of the year nineteen eighty four. When his twenty weeks were up, he was transferred to an office in Savannah, Georgia. After he was settled and had convinced the Government that he was a true agent, he contacted my father and told him to relocate to a city called Augusta, Georgia. That is where it all started. My father and Paul Edgar built their empire from there."

40

No more than three hours later, the man of the hour, agent Paul Edgar was asked to fly into New York. A car was waiting for him at LaGuardia, and from there, they drove him to the federal holding facility where they had Amil. Paul Edgar stepped from the passenger seat of an unmarked sedan inside an underground parking deck. He was escorted straight to a service elevator, dressed in a suit and London fog trench coat.

Fifteen minutes later, he was escorted upstairs through a private door. Inside the room, all the lights were out, and there were at least a dozen more agents standing around the all glass interrogation room looking at Amil and the other four agents inside.

Paul greeted another big wig federal agent, he was senior FBI official, and with a name like Richard Thorne, he had to be a pain in the ass. He shook hands with the older agent. "Good morning, sir."

"Good morning," Richard Thorne responded back.

He folded his arms across his chest, turned back towards

the wall of glass, and looked at Amil, but he addressed Paul. "Do you know the young lady in there?"

Paul turned and looked inside. He squinted and went through his memory bank. "Not personally," he said, "but she's Amil Walker. I have several photos of her because of the big case we had in Florida."

Richard Thorne was a red neck, and it showed in his skin complexion. He never looked at Paul, and instead he kept his eyes straight on Amil. Then he said, "As of now, she has a story to tell that sounds very interesting and very believable. Almost like another government conspiracy, I'd say."

Paul Edgar's eyebrows bunched together, then he said, "I don't quite understand, sir."

"Inside this room," Richard Thorne said and pointed. "Are two of our best intelligence agents and two interrogation specialists who just got enough information on you to send you to prison. Now, this young lady said that you and her father started out together years ago, and when her father tried to pull away from you, you put a case on him in ninety-three because you thought he would spill the beans. However, you didn't know that he was gonna reveal the secret to his daughter."

"I'm willing to take a lie detector test, sir. This is totally out of hand." He put his hands on his waist, looked through the glass at Amil, and shook his head in disgust.

They stood silent for moment, then Thorne said, "It's all coming together against you, Edgar. And I'm not taking anyone's side here, but she also said that you were the one that planted several kilos of heroin in the limousine at LAX, just so you could make the bust, because you told her you needed to move up to a senior FBI official."

Paul Edgar couldn't believe his ears, then small beads of sweat formed on his forehead and eyebrows. Every other agent in the half-lit room was watching Edgar.

"How did she get your phone number?"

"I haven't the slightest idea, sir." Paul was pouring sweat now, and he wiped his sweaty palms on his pants. His eyes darted back and forth.

"From this young lady's truthful statement and everything that we've heard so far, I'll say this. The odds are against you." He took a breath, turned, and looked Paul Edgar straight in his eyes. "Come clean with me, Edgar."

Paul Edgar looked up towards the ceiling and wiped his face with the palm of his hand. "Jesus Christ," he mumbled. Then he said, "I swear to God, I don't know this woman from nothing more than the case that I've been building."

"Tell me about the double homicide at the warehouse in Denver, the crate of guns and key of cocaine. Now I know you passed the polygraph test on the guy that was found in the trunk, but it's clear that you do know something, Edgar."

"I was out having dinner with my wife—"

"Enough of the bullshit, Edgar." Thorne cut him off and yelled. "Do you know this is big? I mean, really big." He pointed a finger at him; even he'd began to sweat. He calmed down, and finally whispered to Paul Edgar, "She says the two of you are lovers, Paul. And that your hideout is a cabin up in the Colorado Mountains."

"Never." He said truthfully.

"Agents and crime scene crew have already combed the place. Your fingerprints are all over the place. Pubic hairs of yours were found in the bed, and one used condom, Paul, with samples of your semen in it. But the worst part of it all, Paul..." The room fell totally silent for a moment. Then he said, "She claims that she's pregnant by you, Paul."

"Well, the DNA test will clearly prove that she's lying." he responded anxiously.

"It damn sure better."

ALMOST FIVE WEEKS LATER, Amil was released after a non-invasive paternity test during her eighth week of pregnancy confirmed that Edgar had indeed fathered her unborn child. They'd run multiple polygraph tests on her, and she had aced every one of them. Before they let her go, she'd signed several papers on behalf of her family, agreeing that they would never step foot on U.S soil again.

The Feds agreed to cease any and all investigations into her family, and to arrange for her to have an abortion before she left the facility, in exchange for her silence... and her absence.

Amil's trick was simple. She used Sarah Edgar's indiscretion with the fake Ken Taylor to force her to get samples of Paul Edgar's semen. The day she flew back to Denver, Colorado, she picked up the samples and went straight to some of her personal doctors and had the artificial insemination done. It took a lot out of her, but she got it done, and clearly she got away with it.

When she got to the sidewalk outside of the Manhattan federal holding facility, Amil was dressed in an all-black Nike jogging suit. It was cold, and early in the morning. From there, she took a cab to the airport. JFK was crowded, but that didn't matter. When she boarded her flight, it was a one-way trip to Dubai.

She flew first class, her hair pulled back in a tight ponytail, and her hands were shoved deep inside her jacket pocket. Looking out the window, she smiled as the plane pulled off. Amil looked around the first class section, and to her surprise, she realized that she wasn't alone. She saw Fly sitting on the other side of the aisle next to Iris. They were disguised as an older couple. She smiled, kept it quiet and enjoyed her flight.

A cute blond flight attendant passed her. "Excuse me, ma'am," Amil said. "One bottle of champagne, no matter the price. I got a lot to celebrate here."

EPILOGUE

The excitement in the air was almost palpable as the guests waited in their seats. This day had been a long time coming, and everyone in attendance was ecstatic to be able to share in it. The sun had started to set, providing a dazzling backdrop for an evening wedding.

The inner courtyard of the Khabir family's home was the perfect location for the event. It was secure and private, not to mention, downright gorgeous. Ornate wrought iron chairs with ivory silk cushions arranged in a semi-circle on each side of the cobblestone walkway gave the space an intimate feel. The eight-foot high arch decorated in flowing white silk and organza fabric, stood in front of the beautiful gold fountain in the center of the courtyard. It was an intimate affair, less than twenty of their closest friends and business associates were invited.

As the soft music began to fade, the minister took his place. Although the official religion of the United Arab Emirates is Islam, Christianity and other religions are practiced as well. The minster was a cousin of the Khabir family, who was born and raised in the United States and had recently moved to Dubai.

Papa Bear walked down the aisle with Amil on his arm, and they took their places next to the minister. Papa Bear was dapper in his custom-made steel grey Giorgio Armani tuxedo with a black shirt and black bowtie. He looked out at the people gathered, and a lump formed in his throat. He had always been a loner, and until recently, he had given up on the notion of having a real family.

As promised, Amil was his best woman, and Papa Bear could think of no one better for the job. She was stunning, in a custom haltered black Marchesa tuxedo styled jumpsuit with pink satin lapels and matching five inch heeled satin Manolo Blahniks. She had been living and loving life since the successful execution of her pink plan. The throne was still her seat, and a new pink design was already in the works.

The nine-piece orchestra struck the first chords to "A Ribbon in the Sky," and Iris came down the aisle, glowing in her ivory Alexander McQueen draped chiffon bustier gown. She carried a bouquet of peach colored Sedona Coral roses in front of her. Her eyes sparkled as she felt a kick from her young prince. In only eight more weeks, he would arrive, and she could not wait to meet him.

Smurf was next to walk down the aisle, also in Giorgio Armani, escorting Jamillah, who also wore ivory Alexander McQueen, but her dress was short, with spaghetti straps. Smurf could not hide his smile as he thought about how much his life had changed. He had decided to make Dubai his home, and was now a partner in a chain of luxury resorts throughout the UAE. With Majid's blessing, he had been dating Jamillah for the last five months, and his heart was slowly opening to love again.

Once Smurf and Jamillah took their places, the music

stopped, and R&B singer Charlie Wilson got up from his front
row seat and went to the microphone near the orchestra.

Butterflies is what I feel inside,
And every time is like my first time...
And I can never find the perfect words to say,
You're the perfect girl, you were made for me...

As Charlie sang, Falisa emerged from the house and made
her way down the aisle. She was breathtaking in a blush
colored silk double-layered Chantilly lace gown with an
embellished bateau neck by Monique Lhuillier. She held on
tight to Fly as he walked her down the aisle wearing a black
Tom Ford tuxedo with a steel grey shirt and neck tie.

Fly walked tall, without the use of a cane. His new high tech
prosthetic leg looked and functioned like a real limb. He was
now able to walk without the slightest limp, and even enjoy a
nightly run along the Sienne River in Paris. As far as Fly was
concerned, the timing couldn't be better. He knew that there
would be nothing to stop him from running after his son, and
all of the other children he planned to have with Iris.

Papa Bear gasped at his first sight of Falisa in her dress. He
couldn't get over how beautiful she was, and the look of love in
her eyes almost brought him to tears.

Amil sobbed openly as she watched her mother walk down
the aisle with her brother. She thought of all that Falisa had
endured to get to this moment, and her heart was just over-
whelmed with joy for her mother. Through prison, sexual slav-
ery, paralysis, heartbreak and betrayal, she had made it, and
she deserved this day, this happiness, and this life.

You're everything,
Oh, baby, you are...

Charlie ended the song as Falisa reached the front. Like a

true mother, she went straight over to comfort Amil. After wiping her daughter's tears and kissing her face, she turned to her son and kissed him on the cheek.

Fly hugged his mom and then hugged Papa Bear, who took his place beside Falisa. Fly walked over to his sister and stood next to her. The siblings held hands as they watched their mother unite in holy matrimony to the man who had shown them both what a father really is.

The minster began the ceremony with a prayer, followed by a few words on the sanctity of marriage. Falisa and Papa Bear then exchanged their vows and placed diamond studded platinum bands on each other's fingers. They were pronounced husband and wife, and finally Papa Bear was able to kiss his bride.

After the ceremony, everyone moved to the 30-foot wide tent for the reception. The newlyweds spent the next few hours dining and mingling with their guests, followed by dancing under the stars, which were visible through the clear roof of the tent.

The magical evening ended with a spectacular fireworks show, courtesy of Fly and Iris.

The guests began to leave after the fireworks display, and soon, only Papa Bear, Falisa, Amil, Smurf, Fly, Iris and the Khabir family were left. Papa Bear and Falisa thanked the Khabirs for their hospitality, and then hugged and kissed the children before getting into their waiting Bentley. They were going to Tahiti for their honeymoon, and from there, they would visit the Ivory Coast, followed by an extended stay in Paris so that Falisa could help Iris with their new grandson. They had been in hiding for so long, that now they wanted to go everywhere and see everything.

As the car pulled off and headed toward the airport, Falisa snuggled against Papa Bear and sighed.

He put his arms around her and kissed her forehead. "What's wrong baby?"

"Nothing is wrong, my love," she said. "For the first time, in a long time, everything is all right. I would even say, perfect."

THE END...

AN AMERICAN HUSTLER

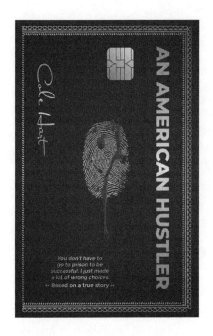

I never had intentions to become a drug dealer, especially at the age of thirteen--just being honest. I had one of the meanest mamas in the neighborhood, who made me go to church almost every Sunday. I had to sang in the Jr. Choir, I'd been baptized, and was a member of a church called Williams Memorial CME on Fifteenth Street. Just across the street is where I stood in line, faithfully, at Shiloe Community Center for our free cheese, powdered milk, honey and most importantly, our monthly Food Stamps.

I wanted to be a football player growing up, but for some apparent reason, my mama didn't think I was tough enough or that I would get hurt. While growing up in a poverty-stricken city such as Augusta, and living in one of the worst neighborhoods, you had only a few options. Either you was going to be a boxer, play football, or be a damn good hustler. Even though the city had produced a few NBA players and rappers, your chances were still slim to none.

Still, I never had intentions on being a drug dealer. I was doing just fine drawing pictures of cartoon characters on my bedroom wall. I was obsessed with picking up soda and beer cans and selling them at the aluminum recycle company on Old Savannah Road. We hunted squirrels and robins with BB guns and sold them to the lady down the street for a dollar. That was my hustle, I guess.

My intentions on being a drug dealer were nonexistent, but this would be the last time our lights and the water would be disconnected at almost simultaneously. I was sure my mama was oblivious to what I was going through mentally. In school, I was ridiculed for various reasons; going to school musty, wearing hand me down clothes that my Mama had gotten from the rich white people that she worked for on the Hill, I also got joked on by the older guys in my neighborhood because they said that my mama didn't know who my daddy was. Maybe, all of this had taken a toll on me.

Then, one day, something clicked mentally; almost similar to someone flipping on a light switch on the wall... And from there, all I could remember is my mama saying, *Whatever you do, just be the best at it.*

This is a powerful story of drug addiction, redemption of overcoming the life of crime and the judicial system all together, Jarvis Hardwick AKA National Bestselling author, Cole Hart, has finally pinned a riveting and unputdownable story of his life

Coming Soon...

Made in the USA
Columbia, SC
10 December 2024

48945699R00124